Tonics

and

Turning Points

Astoria Wright

Faerie Apothecary Mysteries
Book 7

Tonics and Turning Points

Copyright © 2019 by Astoria Wright

Published by Novelwright Press, LLC
http://www.novelwright.com

Cover Art by Viyiwi
https://www.flickr.com/photos/viyiwi/

Edited by 529Books
http://www.529books.com

Table of Contents

Map of Moss Hill

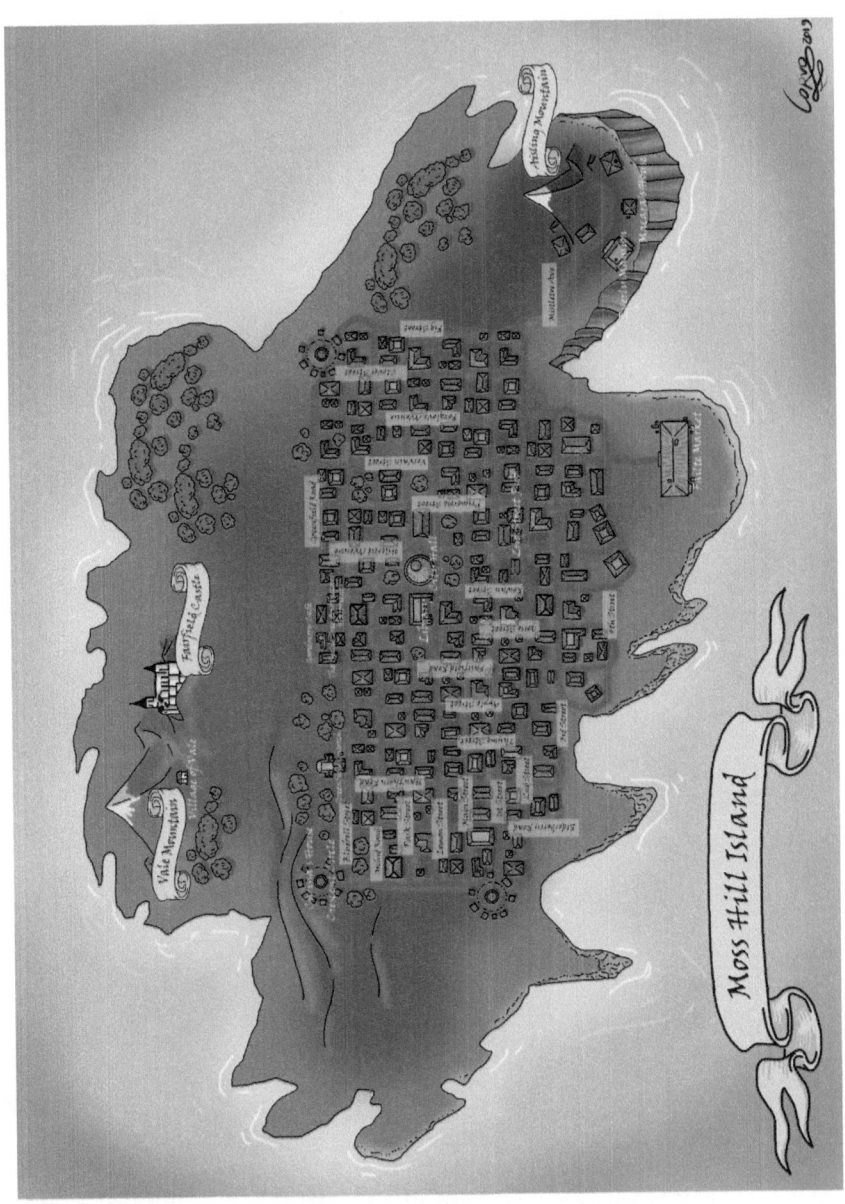

Chapter 1

Wedding Bells and Death Knells

Seeing a bride on her wedding day was not the worst sign that a relationship was doomed. Other signs existed that were much worse: an omen of death, for example.

In her bedroom on the second floor of her home in the neighborhood of Crescent Circle, Carissa Shae admired her bridal gown in the mirror. A clip of gold leaves held auburn hair in a thick, curly bun. The hairstyle made her ears look pointier, which, as a half-elf, she loved.

The gown was the eye catcher, a fairytale style, with a short train. A floral-embroidered bodice accentuated her hourglass figure. A see-though lace top scattered white roses over her neck and ran down the length of her arms. She'd opted for a human-made gown, but there was a faerie-touch about it, as a pair of sprites sprinkled faerie dust over it to make it shine at all the right angles.

Carissa's smile widened at the sight of it, until a distant black dot in the mirror came into focus behind her. In the reflection of her window, just outside her garden, a large, red-eyed dog stared up. Did she see it correctly?

She swirled around. The carefully placed faerie dust flew so that the sparkles on the dress became a twirl in the air.

The tinkling sound of angry faeries filled the room. Cynth and Chaos had not finished decorating the gown. The boy faerie, Hiya, who'd been skipping on the windowsill instead of helping with dresses, stopped. Both hands out, he pressed his nose against the glass. The moment Chaos noticed, she stopped Cynth's angry fist with her hand and pointed. The nature faeries followed Carissa as she peered outside.

Perhaps it was just a dog, a common breed belonging to one of the neighbors. Maybe she'd seen the eyes wrong. A trick of the light or wedding-day nerves playing with her mind. *That was it.* Carissa prayed that was it.

But the red eyes met her again. An unmistakable dread shot through Carissa. She shivered. The half-elf in her felt the magic in her blood stirring. The part of her that was human sent a danger signal through her brain: *The Dog of Death.*

A harbinger of death was not what she wanted to see on her wedding day.

Downstairs, the door slammed open with a bang. Carissa jumped, and the part of her that was a member of an ancient faerie race, the Tuatha de Danann, readied a cloud of mauve-colored magic, which began to form at her fingertips. The intruder made her way upstairs as Carissa turned to the door.

Entering the room, a petite bean tighe, otherwise known as a female leprechaun, said, "Good morning." She did not flinch when she saw Carissa armed with her magic. Instead, she set her sewing basket down on the nightstand and said, "My, what a case of nerves if I ever saw one! You haven't got frozen toes this morning, have you?"

Carissa let go of the breath she was holding and the cloud dissipated around her fingers. She replied, "It's '*cold feet*,' and no, that's not it." She looked out the window again.

The dog had disappeared.

Holly followed her gaze, walking up to the window and peering down. "What is it, then? You look like a spirit."

"A ghost, you mean. And yes, I am *that* frightened."

"If I'd seen this hemline before, I'd say the same. Honestly, you should have come to Barnaby and me sooner. We'd have fixed this right up for you instead of making adjustments on your wedding day." Holly strung a white string through her needle and knelt on the floor.

"I'm sorry, Holly. Between returning home from Hy Brasil, running the apothecary shop, overseeing the building of our new home on Mount Vale, and weeding out the last of the unseelie, I've barely had time to pick out the wedding dress, much less have it tailored."

"Don't mention the unseelie. Talking about evil faeries on your wedding day.... What do you want to cause bad luck for at such a time as this?" She strung the thread over and under the fabric while Carissa tried her best to stay still, all the while fighting the panic building beneath layers of lace and satin.

"I wouldn't have except...." Carissa looked back at the window.

"Except what?"

"I'm sure I just saw the Black Dog of Death."

Holly looked up sharply. "Ow!" She stuck herself with the needle. Bringing her finger to her lips and rising to her feet, she walked to the window. She was just able to see over the ledge. "Where was it?"

"Just there." Carissa pointed at the road. "It looked up at me."

"You're sure it was the hound?"

She nodded. "I've seen it twice before, and both times someone died."

"Mercy! Did it howl?" Holly asked.

"No."

"Well, that's one thing in our favor." Holly paced around the room.

Carissa gripped the window ledge. The nature faeries took to the air above her. "Who do you think it's come for?" she asked.

"There's no way to tell. Have you got a talisman or something for protection?"

Carissa touched the circular, herb-filled locket she'd worn since childhood. "The one my mother gave me. I wear it all the time."

"It might help. Your mother's part Tuatha de Danann. If you have anything stronger, it might be better."

The nature faeries, led by Chaos, raced out of the room. Carissa noted it with curiosity but didn't call them back. When Chaos got an idea in her head, there was no talking her out of it. Whatever purpose had sent them flying, it was best to let it play its course.

"You know, the mind does sometimes make us see things."

"I saw it," Carissa insisted.

Holly held her palms up with the needle still in one hand. "All right. I believe you. I'll tell Macara. Then you'll have two Tuatha de Danann on the case."

"Raven is back?"

"She says she just happened to be passing through, but she doesn't fool me. She's come especially for your wedding, my dear, I'm sure of it."

Holly went back to the dress and Carissa went back to standing still. Carissa bent slightly, lowering her voice, "I don't want our guests in danger. Holly, should I postpone the wedding?"

"And waste my emergency sewing handiwork? Oh, I'm sorry to make light of it, but you've said yourself you've spent weeks searching for unseelie in Moss Hill. Even if you've missed any, I think it's best to leave it to Macara or Jane today. Or better yet, call on Alden. If a grim reaper can't stop an omen of death, I don't know who can. Now stand up straight and hold still."

Carissa straightened and looked back in the mirror. The window was clear of any sign of trouble. She nodded. "You're right. I'm sure Alden already knows and is handling the problem. I'll summon him before the ceremony, just to be sure."

Nan's voice called from downstairs, "Cari, are you ready yet? The mayor's car is here to take us to the church."

Holly cut the thread and stood. "There. All done. You go ahead with your grandmother. Barnaby and I will be there soon. And I'll make you a tonic to calm your poor nerves." She patted Carissa's hands. "Everything will go well, you'll see."

Holly passed the nature faeries on her way out of the room. The three sprites levitated a box using their faerie-dust magic. It floated to Carissa's fingertips. With a curious upraised brow, Carissa took the offering in both hands. She lifted the lid and recognized the coiled seashell with the glowing pearl in the middle.

"The Talisman of Tethra? No. Chaos, you know I'm not supposed to use this. Alden warned me and Raven would kill me herself if she knew I'd used it."

Chaos signed with her hands the waving motion of a ship at sea, a fighting motion, and, finally, a fake death scene. It was a re-enactment of events on their recent voyage on the *Scuabtuinne*. The whole ship had witnessed the talisman leading to Niall Shae's death, indirectly. The prophecy that someone would die via the talisman had been fulfilled then—or so Carissa thought. Alden believed it would cause another death still, but he was overly cautious in nature.

If she wore this today, would it save someone from the hound's omen? Or would it give merit to the warning the dog of death had given?

"Holly did say a more powerful talisman would be better." Carissa reasoned aloud. Chaos gave her a thumbs up. Hiya and Cynth nodded.

"Carissa!" her grandmother called.

"I'll be down in a second!" Carissa called back. She stared into the glowing pearl until a blueish tint reflected in her eyes. Like an ocean wave, a sudden calmness washed over her. Holding the talisman, she felt strong enough to continue with the ceremony. She gave in to Chaos's suggestion.

She took her mother's pendant off. Slipping the Talisman of Tethra necklace over her head, she tucked it under the collar of her dress and said, "I suppose this is something old and borrowed—good luck for a wedding, right?"

Chapter 2

Altar-cation

Snow flurried into whirlwinds controlled by Chaos. The dancing snowflakes matched the rhythm of the butterflies in Carissa's stomach. The waves of calmness had subsided into a numbing sense of dread lingering in the background. Carissa breathed the winter air in, but the cold sent a chill down her spine.

Hiya and Cynth were too busy throwing snowballs and faerie dust to join in Chaos's decorative spirit. At the top of the church steps, Maren Raines, Carissa's best friend, admonished the nature faeries with *"stop-it"* and *"come here"* and, finally, *"I'm going to count to three!"* They responded by hitting her square in the face with snow. It dripped in a watery sludge down her crimson bridesmaid dress. She uttered a startled cry that provoked the chiming sounds of faerie laughter. It took a flick of faerie dust from Chaos's fingers before they quit their antics. After rubbing their stung bottoms, Cynth and Hiya air-dried her clothes with faerie dust by way of apology.

Nan hurried past Carissa and Maren to check last-minute details inside the church. Carissa took one last look around the churchyard before she started up the stairs. There were no signs of trouble, except a gasp from Maren, which caused her to tense. She almost asked what was wrong, but then caught sight of Maren's smile.

Clasping two hands together, Maren crooned, "Cari, you look like an angel!"

Carissa relaxed. Her nose and cheeks must have been red from the cold, and her white, hooded cape, covered the true beauty of her gown, but she took the compliment with a smile. Carissa wrapped her arms around Maren's lace-covered shoulders, hugging her best friend. When they pulled away, Maren's eyes watered. Carissa had no handkerchief to give her.

But Maren pressed a finger to the corner of her eye and kept her composure. "I'm all right. I am all right," she repeated for good measure. Her voice cracked as she added, "I'm just so happy for you."

Carissa sensed the *"always a bridesmaid"* undertone in Maren's voice. Weddings brought up Maren's fears of ending up alone. Carissa couldn't bring herself to feel bad for her friend, though, because she knew something Maren did not. Far from being afraid of commitment, Reginald Smith, Maren's reddish-brown-haired English boyfriend, who had months ago shunned the glasses and khakis of a tourist and donned the suit and tie of Mayor, had settled into life in Moss Hill and planned to propose on Christmas Day. If she wanted to keep that secret for now, though, Carissa would have to stop grinning like a fool every time her friend mourned her unmarried status. So, she gave her a reassuring smile and Maren smiled back, more genuinely this time. She put a hand on Carissa's back and gently guided the bride indoors.

The empty church put a rest to Maren's self-pity. Carissa's doubts about the day dwindled, though they did not die down entirely. Hiya and Cynth's shenanigans ceased, and their jaws dropped on glimpsing the main room. The welcome sign, the flower baskets, and the flickering flame of lanterns down the aisle set the stage for a romantic, winter wedding. The same crimson and pearl-white roses surrounding the sign lay strewn down the center aisle up to the pulpit and across the full-length vertical windows. An archway of vines, tall and towering, stood over the scene where Carissa and Cameron would soon take their vows.

Chaos, less prone to sentimentality, saw room for improvement. Sprinkling her faerie dust on the flowers, she added a gold sparkle to the tips. Then she set to work on the lantern by the sign so that it hovered near the words: *Cameron Larke + Carissa Shae: Wedding Guests Please Sign In.* Hiya and Cynth raced up and down the aisle, haphazardly adding their faerie dust so that Chaos stomped her feet midair and set about fixing their mistakes.

The sound of a man clearing his throat alerted Carissa and Maren to Father Quinn's presence. The priest, with a face too young looking for the hint of gray in his hair, walked toward them from the hallway. He reached out to take both of Carissa's hands.

"You look stunning."

Carissa smiled. "Not as lovely as this room."

"Ah, yes, that was the work of your groom and his party of helpers."

"I sent Reg the color scheme and your choice on the flowers," Maren added. "He said they'd take care of the decorations, but I had no idea he'd do such a breathtaking job."

Father Quinn leaned forward as if sharing a secret. "They did start, but a certain elf-artist and his wife sent them home early and finished the work themselves."

Carissa chuckled. She knew the unnamed elves were Fenigar and his wife, Hela. Asked for or not, Hela would have offered her opinions on the décor. Even with a baby at home, she still found the time to involve herself in Fen's work. Fen was a multi-talented elf-bard who wrote, sang, painted, drew, and built homes beyond comparison with any other artist in Moss Hill—or the wider world—as Carissa knew it. In fact, he was the architect of her dream home, which should be ready by the time she and Cameron returned from their honeymoon.

"The bride's room is ready for you and your maid of honor." Father Quinn held out a note in a sealed envelope simply labeled *"Carissa"* in extravagant penmanship. "And this is for you."

"Thank you." Carissa took the envelope and walked with Maren toward the room to await the ceremony.

She hadn't realized Cameron knew calligraphy, but a love note on her wedding day made everything feel right with the world again. It was even scented with the signature ocean-breeze cologne Cameron had started wearing since their recent sea-faring adventure. In the bride's room at the end of the hallway, Holly, Tabitha, Nan, and Carissa's mother showered her in hugs and questions about her last-minute preferences for the reception hall decorations.

"You wanted the rose-folded napkins, right?" Tabitha asked. The tylwyth teg changeling woman had changed from her usual pointed ears and green skin tone to a more human-like appearance for the wedding. Carissa had told her that wasn't necessary, but Tabitha so desired to fit in that she used her changeling abilities often, sometimes changing right in front of others. She didn't seem to realize that was disturbing in itself.

"I hope you got those in crimson, dear, the white ones blend in with the plates," Holly said.

"Hush, both of you. It's up to Carissa, but you have to decide soon, they're already preparing at the Rose Garden," her mother said.

Chaos flew through the open door and in front of the elder Mrs. Shae's face to sign her disapproval of the mess Hiya and Cynth were making in the main room.

Her chiming was interrupted by Maren speaking through the doorway. "It's crimson rose-folded napkins. Now give her a minute, will you, please?"

"Where are we going?" Tabitha asked with bewildered eyes as Maren pulled her out of the room.

Tonics and Turning Points

"Carissa has a love note from Cameron, and I'm sure she'd like to read it alone. Besides, the nature faeries are doing who-knows-what to the decorations, so we'd better undo their damage before the guests arrive."

Carissa gave a grateful smile as Maren winked at her and led the two out. Her mother put a hand on her arm and kissed her cheek. Then, she, too, left the room. Carissa held Cameron's note to her chest, closed her eyes, and let the mix of magic and love surrounding her heart swirl and settle from excitement to joy. One moment to herself was all she needed to compose herself.

Holly interrupted the minute by opening the door to say, "About that tonic, I've got it ready for you whenever you need it."

Chaos floated back inside. She crossed her arms and pouted, not even bothering to explain why she was angry as she sat on Carissa's shoulder. Hiya and Cynth were getting to her, probably. It didn't matter, as she was soon curious about the note Carissa opened. A moment alone might be impossible, but at least Chaos allowed her to silently read the words to herself.

Cari,
Congratulations on your wedding day. I wish you nothing but happiness—'til death do you part.
Maeb

The note lit in flames. The ash disappeared before it could hit the floor, proving that it had been enchanted. Someone had left the note for her as a threat. Eying the tonic on the vanity, Carissa opened the lid and took a deep gulp. She needed a calm head to think things through.

Maeb, the blot in her family line, the leader of the unseelie, was dead. Tuatha de Danann were powerful, but even one of them couldn't send a note from the grave. Not without an accomplice. Her villainous cousin, Niall Shae, had been Maeb's most devout follower. But he, too, had died. The unseelie were gone from Moss Hill. So, who could have left her the note?

Holly's tonic began working on Carissa—a little too well. She placed a hand on her head, feeling oozy. But that wasn't all. Her lungs felt afire as if the air had left the room. Something was deathly wrong.

Struggling to breathe, Carissa managed to make one last request of Chaos. "Summon Alden."

Then, Carissa fell to the floor, and the world around her went dark.

Chapter 3

Honey Mourning

"Where am I?" Carissa clutched her head.

The room came into focus. She held her hand up, peering through her fingers at a fireplace, lit and blazing. The heat, instead of warming her, stung at her nerves, jolting her into awareness that she was freezing. Not just cold, Carissa felt a chill gripping deep into her core. *Cold as death*, she realized.

She pushed herself up, her fingers digging into a shaggy rug. It was white, soft, and familiar, and not a rug at all but her cape. Carissa did not hesitate to drape it around her shoulders. Standing, she looked around. Hardwood floor, a circular window pain, knotted wood walls that were charming though rustic, it all looked familiar. For a second, she thought Cameron had brought her to their new home on Vale Mountain. But there was something wrong. The room was wrong, or her perception of it. It felt like a dream.

In the eerie glow of the flame, she saw a shadow move. She twisted to look but no one was there. So, she stood.

Her fingers traced the leaves carved into the enchanted wood of the mantle. The faerie fire turned white, and, though her hands could feel the heat as she held them over the flame, Carissa still felt cold. She wrapped her arms around her and walked to the window. Outside, gnarled trees stood tall against the backdrop of a gray sky.

Leaving the window, she faced the room. An armchair, a sofa, a table, a bookcase, all bare and empty and beautifully carved with the natural look of fae-artistry, taunted her with their familiarity.

This was her new home—and it wasn't.

"I'm dead, aren't I?" she asked whoever was with her in the dim room. She could see no one but knew she wasn't alone. She waited.

A minute passed and then a sad, somber voice came from the sofa chair in the corner. "It hurts, doesn't it?"

Carissa spun around, trying and failing to summon her magic. "Who are you?" she asked, fearing she knew the answer. Even though the voice sounded too close for comfort, Carissa couldn't see anyone.

Her hands attempted to summon magic to her fingertips again, but there was nothing. Her heart felt frozen. It had stopped beating. She knew that instinctively. And, as long as that was true, no magic would pump through her veins.

That meant she had no defense against the woman before her, who stood and stepped into the light. She was tall. Long, black hair, eyes like emeralds, pale skin, and a smile that would terrify a grim reaper, this woman personified death.

Carissa looked the woman up and down. The hair, eyes, and skin were all different than Carissa's, but her face had a similar structure. Despite not wanting to admit it, she acknowledged the resemblance. Memory of passages she'd read further linked the woman's face to a description of her great, great grandmother—the Tuatha de Danann—who had gone astray.

The woman spoke, "No magic, no faerie, no family, and no precious human husband to spend a hundred years with, give or take." She walked to the window, her reflection somehow more frightening than her person.

Carissa would not be intimidated. In a stronger voice, she repeated, "Who are you?"

"I know what you're feeling. Scared. Confused. Angry. And cold, oh, that terrible cold. I've felt all of that, too," the woman continued.

"If you do not tell me who you are, I will walk out that door. And I will fight you to the end of time if I have to, to get back to Moss Hill."

"Such fire. Such a shame." She *"tsked"* and shook her head. Then she smiled again, seating herself on the sofa and extending a hand for Carissa to sit beside her.

Carissa refused.

The woman continued, "Very well, I will tell you anything, starting with my name, which I'm sure you already know, since you received my note."

"Maeb," Carissa said.

The woman smiled.

"Yes, child. Now you see. It's all coming clear to you, isn't it?"

"You brought me here. You conspired to kill your own great-granddaughter?" Carissa attempted to reach any part of Maeb that cared.

Maeb clucked her tongue. "You killed your cousin, perhaps not intentionally, but nonetheless, it's true."

"He had a choice. I wouldn't have harmed him except to defend Moss Hill."

"Now, there's the key to it! You have a choice right now. You don't have to die. I won't harm you except that I'm protecting *my* vision for Moss Hill." She held out one hand and then the other, weighing two choices. "And you can either help me bring about that vision or choose to resist and, ultimately, give in to the poison that was in that tonic."

"The tonic," Carissa said, as if just remembering the importance of the substance that had killed her. "You couldn't have put it in the room. Someone living had to do that. Who?"

"What does that matter?"

"I won't have a killer in Moss Hill with my friends."

"You're not the only one with friends in Moss Hill. We might even share a friend or two among the, what do you call yourselves, Mossies? But you're missing the point. Even if you did know who it was, *you're not there* to do anything about it."

"I'll find a way back."

"Yes, you have hope in your grim reaper friend. Let's see how he's doing, shall we?"

Maeb waved a hand. The forest in the window disappeared. In its place, the image of the church came into view, then the hall, then the brides' room. Then, finally, the vision rested on Carissa herself, lying on the white carpet with a skeletal figure standing over her.

* * *

"Carissa? Are you all right?" Kailey Shae rushed into the room as Alden shifted from grim reaper to human form.

Holly entered a second later, a look of terror transformed her expression as she kneeled at Carissa's side. Alden knelt, too. Holly asked, "My god, you're not here for her soul, are you?"

Concern steeled Alden's expression.

"A reaper goes where death or magic calls him," he said.

"I knew something was wrong. I could feel it in the air," Kailey Shae stared at her daughter's form. Though there were no tears, she was a person knocked breathless.

Holly checked for a pulse, but Alden sensed her spirit with just a hand over her heart.

"She's still alive," he said.

"Barely if she is," Holly said.

Chaos pointed frantically to the tonic Carissa had set back on the vanity table. She motioned as if guzzling the liquid down.

"She drank this?" Kailey snatched the tonic from the table.

Chaos nodded. Then she pointed at Holly and signed some more.

Tonics and Turning Points

"My tonic? No, that's not mine. The one I made is in my purse." Holly reached for the bottle, which Kailey handed over without much attention. The concerned mother kept her eyes on Carissa and Alden.

"We'll figure out who's to blame later. Can you save my daughter?" Kailey looked at Alden with a mix of hope and fear in her eyes.

Alden closed his eyes and placed both hands above Carissa's chest. A black mist formed over her frame. Like a storm cloud, electric sparks zapped Alden's fingers back.

Kailey's eyes welled. "I must get Dorian," she said, hurrying away.

With Kailey gone and Alden still trying in vain to use his magic on Carissa, Holly examined the contents of the tonic. She shook the bottle. Chaos leaned on Holly's shoulder, peering at the tonic as it swirled a silvery gray and settled back to clear within seconds.

"Ow, your pinching me," Holly said as the sprite's fingernails dug into her.

The sprite released her, but the fear in her face remained.

Holly's sharp tone softened. "Don't worry. I can get this to the apothecary shop and figure out what's in this concoction. Then, maybe I can save her."

Chaos grabbed hold of Holly's sleeve as if she'd taken issue with the word "maybe."

Holly didn't have time to discuss it. She jumped back as the door slammed hard enough against the wall to leave a dent. The wedding party quickly filled the room, with Cameron at the helm. Hiya and Cynth entered, too, wailing and trying to shake Carissa awake. They were soon displaced by Cameron, who rushed to his bride.

"Cari?"

"She's alive," Alden said again for Cameron's sake.

Pulling her into his arms, he touched her cheek, felt for breath, and cradled her head. He looked at Alden with heart-breaking hope. He asked, fighting tears, "Wha-what happened?"

"She's been poisoned." Holly held up the tonic. Throwing a cape over her shoulders, she headed to the door, adding, "Don't worry. I'll examine the contents and, hopefully, find a cure."

"I'll come, too," Maren said.

"You'll only be in my way," Holly argued.

"Don't be stubborn. I've been at that apothecary longer than you." Maren followed her out.

"Leave us, please." Dorian waved away the bridesmaids and guests.

The nature faeries refused to leave. They settled on the floor beside Carissa. Reg, as best man, stayed, too, kneeling beside Cameron. He put a hand on his shoulder as a comforting gesture.

Dorian shut the door and wrapped his arms around his wife. "Is there nothing you can do?" he asked Alden.

When Alden did not respond, the nature faeries tried with all their might to resuscitate her. Fists and faerie dust hit her chest to no avail. Alden looked curiously past them.

"What is it? Have you thought of something?" Cameron asked.

Alden pointed to a hint of a gold chain sticking out of the neckline. A faint bluish-gray glow pulsated in a rhythm like the beating of a heart at her chest. It dimmed more each time.

Carissa's heartbeat, if that's what it was, was slowing.

Chapter 4

Something Old

The scene in the window faded. Carissa sat on the edge of her chair. The branches of the dead elms swayed, and a light snowfall began, but now she knew this place by name. "This is the borderland between life and death: The Gates of the World Beyond. I can see why I'm here, but why are you?" Carissa asked.

There was a sparkle in Maeb's eye as she answered, "It's not so easy to kill a Tuatha de Danann."

Carissa held back a shudder. She wouldn't let Maeb know how the tone of her voice had raised goosebumps on her arms. Maeb might have been flattered. So, Carissa focused on whatever information she could glean from Maeb's hubris.

"Then, your body is preserved somewhere in the human realm or the Otherworld?" Carissa pondered.

Maeb sighed. "My body was beautiful, as you can see in the image of me you see before you. But that's gone."

"Then what is tying you to the living?"

"A vessel contains a part of my soul and a sliver of my magic."

"A vessel that is here in Moss Hill?" Carissa asked.

It had to be on the island. It was the only way that Maeb would be here. She'd died in Tara, was buried there. So, if her soul was tied to something there, she'd be in the Borderlands in Tara, not in Moss Hill.

Maeb gave a wicked smile. "You are truly my descendent—your mind is quick."

Carissa's mouth twitched. She almost responded with the cliché *"we're nothing alike,"* but that was always what the hero said to the villain. And the villain always found it amusing. Getting riled up would only play into Maeb's twisted plans.

"Where are they keeping your vessel?" Carissa asked.

"Close. Closer than you might think."

"Is it a likeness of you? A statue?"

Maeb wagged a finger. "I consider that personal information."

Carissa had been reading about Maeb. Though she hoped she'd never have to use that knowledge, Maeb was the origin of the unseelie movement. So, knowing her history might help defeat not just her spirit in the Borderlands but the unseelie back home, too.

"You died before Moss Hill was founded. So, whatever it is, it was brought here. But how long ago? Is it something that has been in the town since its inception?"

"You don't care for propriety, do you? Such a lack of manners."

"Just tell me how long you've been in Moss Hill. That's all I want to know." Carissa was determined to get something out of her, even if it was a show of Maeb's power. Part of her said not to risk it; she was already half-dead. She'd rather not make it to full-dead if she could avoid it. A greater part of her wanted information to save her friends from Maeb's conspirator.

Maeb said, "I've only been in Moss Hill a short time, but my heart has been here for many generations, and I'm not saying any more than that."

"A short time, then. That's what I expected. You won't go undetected by our ankou for long."

"You overestimate him."

"And, you underestimate me." Carissa tried summoning her powers again.

Still, she could not feel the surging of her elf-light pumping from her heart. She closed her eyes and allowed her most instinctive magic through. In place of the misty, mauve fog of her Tuatha de Danann magic, her hands shook. She felt a tingling cold race up her arms as if freezing her veins.

An *"agh!"* escaped her lips as she crumpled to the floor. Breathing heavily as Maeb approached her, Carissa fought against the pain. As much as she hated it, the feel of Maeb's hands stroking her hair calmed her muscles. She relaxed despite herself.

"There, there, child." Maeb leaned down to whisper, "Just relax. Sit with me." She stood and waved a hand to the window. "Watch your fate unfold, and then perhaps you'll understand that there is nothing you can do but join me."

* * *

Carissa's body in the human world convulsed.

"Get that necklace off her!" Alden ordered.

Cameron reached for the gold chain. It sparked, sizzling at his fingertips.

"Ow! What is that?" Cameron dropped the chain and clutched his singed fingers. Enough of the talisman was exposed to see it clearly. The conch shell necklace continued to pulsate slow and steady in blue tones.

"That is what's holding her between life and death," Alden said.

"Then leave it on," Dorian commanded.

Alden shook his head. "It's draining her magic to do it."

Cameron lifted Carissa to the chaise, and Kailey adjusted her dress so that she looked like a fair maiden waiting for a storybook ending. But a kiss wouldn't cinch it this time. The talisman kept pulsating.

Reg eyed the necklace. "I've studied every magical artifact in the library and I don't recognize this one."

"Neither do I," Dorian said.

"What is it?" Kailey asked.

Cameron sat on the chaise beside his fiancée. He peered at the conch shell deeper, recognition dawning over him. "That's the talisman from Rhys Dwfen. The...uh...the Talisman of Tethra," Cameron said at the same time as Alden.

Reg clicked his fingers. "I've heard of that. It's from Formorian legends."

"If it's Formorian, then it's unpredictable. It can be used to protect or attack and often does not work as intended," Dorian said.

"I told her to get rid of it," Alden sounded angry. His tone sunk the mood in the room— if such a thing were possible.

"You knew about it?" Cameron asked.

Alden nodded and looked away.

Reg said, "How does Carissa even have it? It was supposed to be lost at sea."

"The washerwoman, a fae we met in Rhys Dwfen, gave it to us to help us defeat Niall Shae," Cameron said.

"She gave it with a warning," Alden added.

"What warning?" Kailey asked.

Cameron's eyes darted across Carissa's face as he searched his memory, "She warned me it would kill someone who was like family to me and, oh god. Cari is my family, married or not, she's everything to me. If I lose her...." He grasped her hand, too overwhelmed to speak. Taking a deep breath, he looked up at Alden. "What do we do?"

As a grim reaper, Alden might know how to bring a person back from the brink of death. Trained as a druid during his life, Alden possessed knowledge kept hidden from other Mossies. The previous mayors believed ignorance was bliss and a way for the fae and human communities to maintain true peace. But the current mayor knew better.

Reginald Smith had come to the island seeking the same knowledge Alden had attained and knew a surprising amount of lore himself.

When Alden didn't speak, Reg said, "The Talisman of Tethra enhances a Tuatha de Danann's power. But you have to be a Tuatha de Danann or a fae strong enough to bare its power. Only, even for a powerful fae it can be dangerous because it has no limits. It can draw out every bit of magic—power the wearer doesn't consciously know how to tap into."

Alden finally spoke up, "But magic is like blood. The body can only produce so much at a time. If it uses what it has, that's it." Alden's face flickered between skeleton and human, adding to the grave expressions shared by all in the room.

Cameron asked, "But if the person can manage to stay alive, the body can produce more. Can't it?"

"Not as long as that thing is on her." Alden pointed at the talisman as if it were a snake around Carissa's neck.

Reg said, "Technically, it did save her life. But it took nearly all of her magic to do it."

"For a fae, losing your magic is fatal. Her human part is what's keeping her alive now," Alden said.

"So, how do we take it off?" Cameron asked.

"It's not about taking it off. It's about reviving her and, if she's half-dead, as I suspect, no living person can do that," Alden replied.

"No. I don't accept that. There has to be a way," Cameron said.

Reg caught Alden's meaning. "Wait—you said 'no living person,' does that mean a dead one can?"

Alden answered, "I might be able to find her. She'll be in the Borderlands—not quite in the World Beyond yet, but no longer in the land of the living. If I can bring her back to the living world, she can control the amount of power the talisman is taking from her."

"What happens if we don't get the talisman off her?" Kailey asked.

Alden's human face looked as ominous as his skeletal form, sallow and sickly, as he replied, "As she is, she's already fated to die. She just won't have a chance of changing that."

"So, you'll go to the World Beyond and find her. We'll try to find a way to get the talisman off her here," Reg suggested.

Cameron agreed. "There has to be something in Carissa's grandfather's books."

"We can scour the Moss Hill historical records at the library, too. They've found whole crates of books and journals since the renovations," Reg said.

Stroking Carissa's hair, Cameron kissed her forehead. Then, he stood. "Let's not waste a second."

Alden placed a hand on Cameron's shoulder. "I wish I could tell you I'll bring her back, but I can't make any promises."

"Just promise you'll try everything you can," Cameron said.

"I'd trade my soul for hers if it would save her. I promise you that." Alden's form faded to the skeletal image of an ankou, then he disappeared into the Borderlands between life and death.

Chapter 5

Something New

Despite the fire that heated no more than the thinnest layer of her skin, Carissa smiled. Holly and Maren's determination to find a cure, Cameron's concern, and Alden's willingness to search for her—they were what warmed her heart. It gave her courage and hope.

"You see? My friends will never give up on me." Carissa looked away from the window. But Maeb was no longer in the sitting room.

The chair to her right, the sofa behind her, the hearth by the fireplace, all were empty. As far as she could see into the other room, it was dark. Taking a deep breath, Carissa tried to stand. She hadn't regained much of her strength but summoned enough willpower to stand.

Alden was on his way here. But he might not find her without help. If Chaos were with Carissa, she could simply have the sprite summon him, but Chaos was, thankfully, still in the living world.

Carissa walked to the window. How did this work? Mirror magic. Mirror magic was something she vaguely recalled reading about in her grandfather's books. She'd seen

Macara and the Tuatha de Danann use them in Hy Brasil, too.

Carissa was having a hard time remembering all the knowledge she'd gained in the last year. Magic just didn't stay in her head—not like the various uses of medicinal herbs. If she had to make a potion to enact a spell, she could do that without a problem.

But magic? Except for her innate skill, of which she had much, she couldn't remember how spells and powers worked. Cameron was better at that, even if he couldn't use it.

If he were here, he'd tell her what to do. What would he say? Carissa put a hand on the glass and tried to recall what they'd read about the magical properties of mirrors. They granted wishes? No, that was jinn magic. Mirror magic worked by…the inner eye, that was it.

She had to envision the person she wanted to talk to. But that person would have to be near a reflective image—a mirror would be the best case. The church room had one, but Cameron and the others were already leaving. Perhaps he could catch a glimpse of her in the car mirrors? No, that would be dangerous. He might swerve and get into an accident.

Alden wouldn't have a mirror, but the Everly mansion had plenty. Large mirrors and the reflective surfaces of antique, gold pieces were displayed in every room. It was her best chance.

She tried for Jane.

"Jane," she whispered into the glass. She had to be quiet, and she had to be quick if she didn't want Maeb to stop her. She closed her eyes. "Please, Jane. You're a druidess. You can feel me speaking to you. I know you can. Look into your mirror. Please, I need you. Just look into your mirror. Now."

Opening her eyes, Carissa gazed intently at the scene in Jane's house. There was her sofa, her coffee table, the edge of the kitchen in the background, the sliding doors to the back yard, where they'd once rescued Alden from another ankou. But no Jane.

There was a gasp. Someone was there. They just were not in view of the mirror.

Varick stepped into the scene. He was dressed in the full dress uniform of a sidhe guard: a long black coat with bronze stripes on his shoulders and wrists and a silky shirt with black beneath it—that might have been his own touch—open just enough to see the hint of the brawny chest beneath it. His blond hair was tied back. His green eyes were sprinkled with tiny specs of gold that meant he was concerned.

"Jane?" His voice was muffled through the glass.

"I feel something. Someone is here with us," Jane said.

"Alden?" he asked.

"No. It's not an ankou. It's...." Jane's face appeared in the mirror. She tucked her long, dark hair behind her ears. The soft, shiny strands framed her face so that her blue eyes seemed especially piercing. The problem was, Jane couldn't see Carissa on her end.

"I'm here, Jane! It's me, it's Cari!" Carissa's whisper grew, but she dare not speak loud enough for Maeb to hear. With desperation in every note, Carissa said, "I can't use my magic. You have to use yours."

As Jane put her hand across the mirror, her druid magic glowed from her palm and Carissa could hear her last word make it through.

"Yours," reverberated on the other side.

Jane and Varick's eyes both widened. Varick stepped closer. "Carissa Shae, is it you?"

"Cari, how?" Jane asked.

Tears stung at Carissa's cheeks, and her words choked in her throat as she struggled not to cry. It had worked! They could hear and see her.

Once she regained control of her breath, she said, "Jane, Varick, I'm stuck in the border between worlds. My soul is still attached to my body, but I'm not there. Maeb won't let me return until her plan is complete."

"Maeb!" Varick's tone was a mix of outrage, fear, and disbelief. "She is behind this?"

"She's behind everything. It was one of her operatives who put the tonic in my room at the church."

Jane asked, "But how? We got rid of all the unseelie. Tabitha screens for changelings, and you and I created a magical barrier around Moss Hill. No unseelie can enter."

"Was there anyone suspicious at the church?" Varick asked.

"Only friends, and the only people I ever see at the church are Mossies."

Varick put a hand to his chin. "I can think of no Mossie who would want you harmed."

"Someone did. Maeb didn't tell me who it was, but...." She hesitated to say it. Carissa didn't want to believe any Mossie would choose to be Maeb's accomplice. She had to say it, though, had to admit that someone in town had poisoned her—though she kept the hope that they did Maeb's bidding unwillingly. "Maeb has an accomplice in Moss Hill. If she's at all truthful, it's a friend and fellow Mossie."

"A mossie? Trying to harm you? I can't believe it," Jane said.

Varick put a hand to his chin, musing. "Perhaps the old Mayor, or the current one. We don't know much about this Reginald Smith."

Carissa couldn't accept that. Reginald was new to Moss Hill, but in his heart, he was as Mossie as anyone. And Maren loved him. Carissa and Cameron—even Chaos—had grown fond of him over the year since Carissa had rescued him from Vale woods.

"We can save our accusations for later," Jane said. "Right now, we have to rescue Carissa. Cari, stand back, I'm going to open a portal. You can step through the mirror to get home."

"No. If I go home any way other than with Alden, I risk breaking my connection to my body. Can you call on him?"

"He is searching for you," Varick said.

Tonics and Turning Points

Jane asked, "You said you're in the Borderlands. Do you know exactly where you are? Perhaps we can get a message to him."

"I think I'm in the house that Cameron commissioned Fen to build for us, but Maeb has it protected. I don't think he can get in."

"Maeb has her powers? Of course, if she's in the Borderlands, so she's still somehow attached to the world of the living. Do you know how?"

"A vessel of some kind. She wouldn't say what, some kind of object that could hold her magic or soul or both, something like that." She'd actually said "soul and magic," but that wasn't clear since no one truly knew whether the two were or were not the same for a fae. Carissa wished she'd understood it plainly, but Maeb had a way of speaking that sound like riddles.

Jane paced the room. "Maeb is a Tuatha de Danann. If she has been able to restore any of her powers after death, she might be able to overpower a grim reaper like Alden, too. You have to get out. Head across the woods. If you can make it into the church grounds, Maeb should not be able to touch you. We'll send a message to Alden to try to meet you along the way."

Carissa nodded. "I've got it, I'll do my best."

"No, Jane. Carissa, you must not try to cross the woods alone," Varick said. "The sidhe call the Borderlands the Endless Woods. I know only one thing about it. Souls are meant to cross it only one way: toward death."

Carissa looked at Jane for guidance, but her face was as grim as a reaper. There was no choice here.

"I have to try."

The reflection faded. Maeb still hadn't returned, for which Carissa was grateful. She tried walking out of the room, but a magical barrier had been placed there. Maeb had trapped her inside. Carissa looked around for an escape, but she knew the layout. The living room had no exit to the outdoors.

None except the window.

Carissa grabbed the poker from the fireplace and swung at the glass. Any cracks that appeared sealed themselves up within seconds. This would take magic to break. Knowing it was dangerous, Carissa summoned what little magic she had left.

The combined force of magic and thrust shattered the glass. The exertion left her winded but, even as Carissa gulped for breath, she moved forward. There was a wave of dizziness, but it passed soon enough. Taking a shard from the floor, Carissa did not hesitate to pull herself through the window.

She made it outdoors, but only gave herself seconds to recover before starting her journey. Whatever lay in wait for her in the Borderlands could not be worse than staying here with Maeb. For her sake and for that of Moss Hill, she would have to risk it.

* * *

MOSS HILL LIBRARY was filled with students. Those in high school prepared for winter finals while younger ones perused the shelves of the children's section for holiday reading materials. In the very back of the first level were the books not advertised and rarely visited. A partition made it unclear whether the books were available to patrons. Except for a few curious wanderers, Cameron, Reg, and Maren were alone.

Maren had surprised Reg and Cameron by showing up in jeans and an old Christmas sweater, sleeves rolled up and ready to help. "Helping Holly is like babysitting a changeling infant—impossible." Maren had said. So, she sat beside Reg and skimmed books with them.

Cameron searched until his vision blurred. He rubbed his eyes and put a hand to his forehead. Reg stretched in his seat.

Maren sighed. "There's nothing here. Nothing on the talismans, tonics, or anything that would identify who could have poisoned Carissa."

"Keep looking," Cameron said.

Tonics and Turning Points

Reg said, "Okay. What do we know? The tonic was meant to kill. The talisman saved her. Holly is examining the tonic as we speak, so she'll get the ingredients to us when she discovers what was in it. Whoever poisoned Carissa had access to both the ingredients and to the church."

"We're not looking for her killer. We're looking for a way to override the talisman."

"As mayor, I have to disagree. We need to be doing both. Saving Carissa is of first and foremost importance, but if there's an unseelie assassin out there, we have to find him before he strikes again."

"He or she," Maren corrected. "And should we be looking for a cure to the talisman or to the tonic? If the talisman is what's saving her life, maybe we shouldn't take it off until we've cured Cari of the tonic's effects."

Cameron rubbed both hands across his face. "I don't know. It doesn't matter if we can't find anything on the tonic or the talisman. Maybe I should recheck Cari's grandfather's books."

"You've already read them all," Reg said.

"I'll read them again." Cameron slammed the book he was looking through shut.

Maren put a hand on Cameron's back and glanced at Reg. But before either could say any empty words of encouragement, Cameron lifted his hands off his face and started stacking the books for reshelving.

"Cam?" Reg asked.

"We're going about this all wrong. Raz is the one from whom Carissa got the talisman in the first place. He said he doesn't know anything about it, but what if he does? What if he wanted it back?" Cameron stood.

"Wait just a minute." Reg pulled him back into his seat. "Before you start going around accusing friends—"

"Even if he isn't responsible, he might still know something about the talisman," Cameron argued.

"It doesn't hurt to go see him in Vale," Maren said.

Reg said, "Maybe I should go myself. If you keep reading through the books, you might find something on deadly tonics—"

Maren put a hand on Reg's arm and shook her head.

He looked in the direction she was looking. A boy, Timothy Harbridge Junior, was walking by the window of the librarian's office, near enough to overhear.

Little Timmy stopped at the window a second, looking into it. Since the light was off, the window displayed only his own reflection. Nevertheless, Timmy squinted as if trying to see what was there. Then he shuddered and passed by it into the roped-off section where Cameron, Maren, and Reg were seated.

"Hello Cam, Maren, Mr. Mayor," the precocious nine-year-old said. "Mom and Dad were talking about what happened to Cari. I'm so sorry she's sick."

Maren smiled softly, "Thank you, Timmy. But you're not supposed to be in this area."

"Right," Timmy said glancing sideways like he'd snuck into this section more than once before. He turned as if he were going to leave, but then looked back at each of their faces. "She's not just sick, is she?"

"You know, this is something we need to handle ourselves. Sorry, kid," Reg said.

Timmy, despite the remonstrations he would have received from Nan or any of the other librarians, walked to a shelf and pulled out a book, placing it in front of Cameron. "Not sure if this will help but it's full of magic-related illnesses."

Cameron's smile was near chuckling, not the mocking kind adults usually showed to children, but genuine amazement at Timmy's contribution, "Thank you, Timmy."

"You know," Timmy faced Reg, "One day *I* am going to be mayor, and then I'll give everyone in Moss Hill access to all the secret books—as a right of Mossie heritage."

Reg chuckled aloud. "Sorry, my friend, there are no secret books in the mayor's office."

Timmy held his head up high, "There are so. Belkin promised to pass them on to me."

He turned to leave, and he might have made a grand exit just then, except that Nan's voice came from the nearest stacks. "Timothy Harbridge, what have I told you about being in this section?"

Timothy deflated, not enough to sulk, but enough to look like a kid again. "Adults only."

"That's right, and only adults with official Mossie business, which you do not have."

"Yet," Timmy whispered under his breath.

"Scoot," Nan said. She rolled up her sleeves to show she meant business.

Timmy ran off, which caused her to whisper-yell, "No running. And find your mother, I'm sure she's looking for you."

Nan walked up to the table. She was no longer in her gown for the wedding, but in a maroon cardigan and a green pair of slacks. When she walked over, she put a hand to her forehead, not bothering to hide her bloodshot eyes with bags underneath. Her face had been cleared of all makeup. Although she still looked youthful for a grandmother, her age showed in the sadness behind her eyes.

Cameron stood, offering her a seat. "What are you doing here? I thought you were going to stay with Cari?"

She held a palm out, declining to sit. "Kaley is with her, and Dorian is on his way back to Vale. He wants to call an emergency council meeting."

Reg's eyes widened, "He didn't say anything to me. We agreed the mayor would be informed of all council meetings—if not invited."

"I'm informing you now, and I'm sure you're invited if you want to go." Nan rubbed the back of her neck and sighed.

"Are you all right?" Cameron asked.

"I had to come in and do something or I'd go insane."

They were silent a moment, all of them nodding as if to say they felt the same way. Being helpless was more difficult

33

than trying in vain to help, even though their efforts had felt futile from the start.

"We're glad you're here." Maren broke the silence. "Nessa, we just heard from Timmy that the mayor has his own collection of books about Moss Hill's magic and the history that gets passed on from one mayor to the next."

"I'm telling you, I don't have any such collection," Reg stressed.

Maren put a hand on his fingers, "I know. I'm not saying you do." She looked back at Nan, "Is it possible Belkin is holding onto some knowledge that only mayors were privy to in the past?"

Nan tapped her fingers to her chin, thinking a moment. "My husband had a rather large collection of books and journals that he donated to the library, kept under lock and key until recently." She nodded toward the shelves in the roped-off section. "As for books for the mayors' eyes only, it is possible. But I'm afraid I don't remember what's missing from the collection. I wouldn't put it past Belkin to hang onto volumes that are not his to own."

Maren popped out of her seat. "That's all I needed to hear." She took her coat off the chair. "Let's pay the old mayor a visit, shall we?"

Cameron kissed Nan's cheek and gave her shoulder a sympathetic squeeze. "Thank you." Then he turned to Reg, "I think we ought to see Belkin and then join Dorian at the council meeting."

"Oh, yes," Reg said, putting on his coat. "He and I are going to have some words."

Chapter 6

Borrowed Time

The woods were dark, deep, and reminiscent of every other creepy descriptor one had heard about the World Beyond. A bitter chill bit at Carissa's skin. She couldn't run much longer like this. Dropping to a walk, Carissa wrapped her arms around herself. She was panting now. Looking back to judge the distance she'd run, she couldn't see the cabin anymore.

Carissa eyed the surrounding trees to gain a sense of direction. Somewhere in her mind, she recognized this was Vale Mountain, but she'd never seen these woods in the eerie light of the Borderlands. Carissa had no idea if she was walking toward town or away from it. It had to be afternoon in the living world. Aside from that, she had lost all sense of time and space.

The sun, dim as it was here, shone directly overhead. If time translated the same as in the living world, it was around noon. Moss seemed to cover every part of the redwoods and the ground here, so that was no help. She walked toward what she hoped was a path far ahead. If she were in Moss Hill, she could use her elf-light to quicken her step. With the talisman still around her neck, Carissa dared not use any more magic than was necessary.

But she had to see what was happening in Moss Hill. When she came to a thicket, she paused to catch her breath.

Pulling the shard of glass she'd saved from the window out of the pocket of her cape, she used the little magic required to see into the living world. The glass showed Cameron and the others in the library, but there was no hope of gaining their attention. Carissa didn't have the strength.

Plus, she was seeing them from a side view, probably the window of the librarian's office. It was too far off to the side to hope they could see her. Timmy did look up once with an expression that made Carissa moved on. She watched until she felt her magic draining. Then she re-pocketed the shard and rested against the root of a redwood tree. She closed her eyes and breathed in a deep, steady rhythm.

Sounds were different here. At times there was nothing, no birds or animals or people. At other times, the wind whistled in whispers that threatened of a storm coming. And, out of nowhere, thunder occasionally cracked from all directions, close enough to sound like giant redwoods snapping in half. One particularly loud bang shook the tree behind her. Carissa bolted to her feet. The wind seemed to be picking up, and so she had no choice but to make her way toward the path she hoped was a half-mile or less out.

The branches of smaller trees scraped at her legs. She never recalled the trees sitting so narrowly against each other nor the Vale woods stretching endlessly onward. *The Endless Woods,* now the sidhe descriptor made sense.

Where was the clearing? Where was the path to Vale? To Moss Hill? The further she went, the more foreign the landscape.

She stopped at a clearing and turned in a circle. The redwoods, the moss, and even the flowers were the same kind as Vale. So, why did they take on a disorienting appearance? Was it a spell of some type?

Carissa inhaled slow, steady, long. The air stung her nostrils, going in but warmed her going out. If this forest worked like old, ancient magic, she would have to use it the same way she used her innermost powers. There was no choice. Carissa closed her eyes, breathed again, in and out, until she felt the beating of her heart.

Don't think. Just let the magic flow.

She stood. Trying again, this time Carissa walked, less with a purpose and more with hope. She ignored the misleading paths that opened before her.

Carissa thought of home. She pictured picking herbs in her garden, Nan putting on a fresh pot of tea, the scent of Maren's cobblers from Gooseberry bakery permeating her apothecary shop, her regular customers coming in for their tonics.

Tonics.

The thought hit her like thunder just as it thundered overhead and lightning flashed. She thought of the drink that had put her under. Who had given her the poison that had brought her here?

It thundered again, the world shuddered under her feet. It began to shower. The rain stung as if freezing Carissa's skin on impact. Forgetting her magic, Carissa clutched her dress and dashed toward whatever path—real or imagined—might lie ahead.

Had her thoughts done this? Or, was it a coincidence that as soon as she'd thought of a threat the Borderlands provided one? She didn't have time to consider.

With every step, the wind picked up, like a snowstorm out of nowhere. Carissa quickened her pace, running until her breath came out in heaves, and her heartbeat drummed in her ears. All the while, the storm picked up, louder and harsher than before, until the wind drowned out every sound but foreboding thunder.

When she could run no more, she headed for a redwood for shelter. Panic gripped her, adding to her shortness of breath. She felt the world blurring. She fell. But as her hands sunk into the soil, she felt arms wrapping around her.

Thinking it was Maeb, she tried to pull away. But these were strong arms, the arms of a man. They made her think of Cameron—though she didn't see how that was possible. The man lifted her, bundled her into his arms, and carried her away.

"Alden?" she asked.

Carissa tried to get a glimpse of her rescuer, but all she saw was dark clothing, and then the darkness of unconsciousness overtook her.

* * *

"YOU THINK I had something to do with this?" The former mayor, Sean Belkin, looked unsurprised.

With a tea in his hand, in the low light of his fireplace, he appeared ominous. He was no longer hiding his troll features: the wild eyebrows, the bulbous nose, the sallow skin. His hulking figure in the armchair beside the bearskin rug, made him seem more ferocious than he was in reality.

His fall from grace left him vulnerable to suspicion. After all, he had lied to the Mossies, pretending to be human instead of a fae. After a lie like that, no one would ever fully believe he was not unseelie.

Cameron may have been one of the few people who still trusted him. Having been his chauffeur for years, Cameron knew him well. In matters of business, Belkin was shrewd. Money motivated him, but people did, too. Belkin acted where he thought money and Moss Hill's interests intersected, only he'd been wrong about not including the people of Vale. If he had included them and been open about his own fae heritage, life might have gone differently for him.

"We're not making accusations, we just want to save Carissa." Cameron ran a hand through his rich, brown hair and then rested it on the back of his neck. "If you have any magical knowledge or town history that could provide any insight—"

"Town history? What's that got to do with saving Carissa?"

"Maeb is in Moss Hill. We've just heard it from Jane, who was contacted by Carissa on the other side," Maren said.

Belkin gasped, then coughed violently, sputtering his tea over the mahogany, hand-carved coffee table. He set the cup on its coaster and took out a handkerchief. Once he'd regained his voice, he squeaked, "How? Maeb is dead."

"She's in the Borderlands with Carissa. Somehow, something prevented Maeb from moving more than partway into death. We think she has a vessel here that is holding part of her soul," Cameron said.

"I see, I see," Belkin said.

Maren added, "Mayor, Mister Belkin, she has a spy here, a fellow Mossie. Do you have any idea who that might be?"

"A spy," Belkin repeated to himself. Bringing his hand to his chin, he stared into the fireplace.

"Sir?" Cameron asked after a while.

"Rumors. Pure speculation, my boy. I cannot point fingers—that would be dangerous. I have no proof of anything."

Reg sighed, "We know you have books, town history, secret spells, a wealth of information that belongs to the office of the mayor."

"Nonsense. Where did you hear that?"

Belkin seemed to have forgotten that he'd used his handkerchief a second earlier to sop up tea from the table. He raised it to his forehead to dab the sweat from his skin. The dampness registered, and he pulled the 'kerchief away, wet at his forehead and red-faced now.

"Please, sir, this is a matter of life and death," Maren said.

Belkin's eyes fell on Cameron. He studied Reg's face.

"All right. Yes. The books are there, behind the classics."

Belkin pointed to the bookshelf beside the fireplace. Reg stood and examined the books until he found a dummy spine titled *Of Gods and Fighting Men* by Lady Gregory. The shelves slid back and down, revealing an inner row of a dozen or so books. As Reg perused them, Cameron focused on Belkin.

"And, Maeb? Do you have any idea who might be helping her?"

Belkin glanced sideways at Reg, then looked back at Maren and Cameron. "The rumor was that the wealthiest family in Moss Hill was connected to the World Beyond."

Cameron nodded. "The MacAirts or rather the Everlys. Mrs. Everly was the last MacAirt, so they are the modern descendants. Their family's tie to the Tuatha De Danann MacLir is well known."

"Not the MacAirts, my boy. There was another family. I don't recall their names. They left the island to make their fortune in London. They were spies, people said, who were secretly in league with Maeb."

"Unseelie?"

"No, no, they were human. Druids. They saw themselves as superior to humans who had no fae magic in them. Maeb offered a special place for druids when she took over the human and fae realms."

"But, this family left Moss Hill?"

"Driven out, in a way. The Mossies were not very welcoming of their manners. But when they left Moss Hill, they promised that they would return. And, one of them who was a seer, predicted that his great-grandson would eventually bring Maeb back to life."

Maren gasped. "Who? Who here in Moss Hill would do such a thing?"

"Someone who isn't a Mossie," Cameron said. "Someone who is just pretending."

"Who?" Reg asked.

Belkin looked Reg in the eye and nodded. "Who, indeed?"

Chapter 7

From Better to Worse

Carissa stirred. The flicker of a fireplace met her ears and she became aware of the warmth around her. She opened her eyes to see the wooden frame of a cabin ceiling.

"Oh no." She shot up.

A hand stopped her.

At the familiar blue eyes, Carissa breathed a sigh of relief. "Alden, thank goodness. I thought for a second this was Maeb's cabin."

"Rest, you're still healing," Alden said.

"You mean up there or down here?"

"Your body is the same. But the mind can need repair just as much as the body. You went through an ordeal in the woods."

She put a hand to her forehead. "And I dreamed about a funeral. It was on a cliffside, overlooking water. It reminded me of the back yard at your parents' mansion. There were two women there and two men. I couldn't see their faces. But one of the women had a necklace, a tree with gemstones that were shining as if absorbing the rays of the sun."

Alden's eyes drifted past her with a pensive stare at the wooden floor. She scooted closer to him.

Putting a hand on his shoulder, she asked, "Alden?"

He pulled back. "It was just a dream."

He smiled, and though it seemed forced, Carissa didn't pry. Perhaps she shouldn't have mentioned a funeral at his home. She might have reminded him of his own death, and the last thing she wanted to do was cause him pain. So, she went with his explanation.

"But how is it possible for me to dream here?"

"You're half-alive in the Borderlands. Your mind is still connected to a body that tires and dreams of random, meaningless things. You need to rest so your body can heal."

"Maeb said she's still connected to a vessel in the world above. But she's not connected to a body, is she? That would be a centuries-old corpse by now."

Alden's lips tugged down, and his eyes wouldn't meet hers. He stood and threw the last log in his bundle onto the fire. Leaning his lithe frame against the mantle, he stared at the burning wood. His eyes reflected the red of the firelight, and his skin seemed transparent. His skeletal form would scare many, but Carissa knew the man so she felt no fear.

Still, his behavior was so off, she had to ask, "What's wrong?"

He closed his eyes. "I'm so sorry." When he finally lifted his face, there was anguish in his eyes. Carissa's eyebrows knotted. Then a figure emerged from the shadow behind Alden.

Maeb settled a hand on his shoulder. "It's all right, Alden. I know you've grown close to your mark. She's grown on me, too."

So, this was the same cabin she'd left. Looking around, she saw that it was the same, including the window that had been repaired. Alden had brought her back here. To Maeb.

"Why?" Carissa's heart broke. She didn't know why the betrayal hit her so strongly, except that she'd seen such depth of feeling in his eyes before. She wouldn't dare name the emotion, but she was sure he cared for her too much to hurt her like this. Carissa's voice shook as she said, "I trusted you."

Tonics and Turning Points

Alden's eyes welled. "Cari, I—"

"You should be thanking him," Maeb said. "It was a foolish plan on your part to try to escape these endless woods. The only way Alden did it was with my help."

Carissa's eyes would not let Alden's go. "The plan was to find Alden and return to Moss Hill." She studied the emotion on his face with so many questions. Was he doing this against his will? But what about Maeb saying Carissa was his "mark?" Didn't that mean he had been working with Maeb? That he'd targeted Carissa this whole time? Or was the betrayal more recent than that?

Perhaps and most importantly, what did Maeb mean about his crossing the woods with her help? Did she mean just now? Or had he once been in Carissa's situation?

Difficult as it was, Carissa stood. She measured at least two inches below Maeb's towering figure but was determined to make her stand a literal one. She knew from her previous experience that she could not overpower Maeb. But she was done being her prisoner.

Draining or not, she had to use her magic. Carissa closed her eyes and felt her Tuatha de Danann magic stirring from the deepest recesses of her core to her palms. Then, she felt a hand enclose around hers. Her instinct was to pull away. She opened her eyes, ready to attack.

Alden stood in front of her, holding her hand gently, palm to palm. He shook his head. His eyes pleaded.

"Don't, Cari. It'll kill you."

"I'd die willingly for Moss Hill. Up to now, I thought you would do the same."

"He can. He did," Maeb said, taking a seat in her wide armchair.

"I think it's time you tell her your story. Go on. Take a walk in the woods."

Alden looked at her, raising a brow. She batted her hand in the air as if swatting the question away.

"Oh, don't worry about me. I'll be watching through the window."

* * *

"DEAR ME," Holly said sitting opposite Cameron in the big red booth at the front window of Gooseberry café. "And Reg has gone to the council meeting?"

"Who cares about a council meeting! He just told you that a scorned Mossie family is back to take down the town. Priorities, woman." Barnaby sat next to her with his sandwich in hand.

Holly raised an eyebrow, looking her leprechaun boyfriend straight on as she replied, "And, Reg is the priority here. Why do you think he's come to us without Reg? Think about it, Barn."

Cameron looked miserable holding his head in his hands. "Maybe I shouldn't have said anything. I hate what I'm thinking."

"What are you thinking?" Barnaby gave a puzzled expression over his tea.

"I...I can't say it," Cameron sat, defeated.

Holly put a hand on Barnaby's, "Reginald, my dear. He thinks Reginald is part of the Mossie family who has come back to take down the town."

"That's what Belkin hinted at as I was leaving. He grabbed my arm and whispered, *'Would you trust him with your life?'* and he looked at Reg. Thank goodness Reg left before me to drop off Maren at Nan's before going to Vale."

"A kind thing to do. I can't believe Reg would betray Moss Hill." Barnaby shook his head. "That boy has helped us more than once. And he might not be a Mossie by birth, but he embraces the spirit as much—no, *more* than any of us."

Cameron leaned forward from his side of the booth, saying, "Except that Reg fits the description: wealthy, from London. He's the right age, too—two hundred years and three generations later."

Barnaby repeated his words, "Wealthy, from London, even being the right age—that's not enough to convict him, or to convince ourselves that he's guilty."

Tonics and Turning Points

"You might have to accept the possibility," Holly said, sipping her tea.

Barnaby's hands shot out wide, exasperated. "Maren loves him. That girl might be in love with him. Are you going to be the one to hurt her by telling her that?"

"He's right. We can't just blindly accuse him. We need proof."

Holly's eyebrows pulled together. She looked at her shoes, shaking her head. "All right, point taken." She patted Cameron's hand. "You did right to come to us for advice. We'll keep this all hush, hush until we can gather some evidence."

"Thank you. How did you make out on the tonic?"

Holly fumbled through her purse and took out a crinkled list. "The ingredients are the exact ones found in a sleep tonic, even in the same quantities."

"Then it shouldn't have harmed her," Barnaby said.

Holly shook her head. "Some of the ingredients can cause the heart to react or even to stop, depending on the strength of the herbs used or the preparation of the tonic."

"So, the tonic was improperly impaired?" Cameron asked.

"Are you sure you didn't make it?" Barnaby asked, jokingly.

Holly swatted him on the arm. "It's not mine. And it wasn't improperly prepared. That wouldn't have ensured death. No, the maker used magic to enhance the riskier ingredients like the atropa belladonna, which can stop the heart. Some other ingredients, like valerian root, are harmless. But, if magically enhanced, it has the same effect. This was cleverly designed to look like a regular tonic. Only magic would reveal its poisonous qualities."

"A druid fits with Belkin's theory. Were you able to make a cure?"

"It's too complex to counteract the magic in each poison and the interactions between the magically infused herbs makes a cure impossible."

"What about counteracting the magic itself?" Barnaby asked.

"Based on what Macara told me, the talisman used Carissa's magic to counter the effects of the tonic. But, it wasn't enough to get rid of the druidic magic, so the tonic will continue to poison her until it works its way out of her system."

"What if Macara or Raven use their magic to heal her?" Cameron asked.

"The talisman might treat outside magic as an attack. The magic would have to come from within her."

"Thank you for trying." Cameron looked at his wristwatch.

Holly said, "You best be on your way to Vale. The council meeting may have already begun."

"I'm waiting for Macara. She said she'd meet me here."

"I know. She fibbed, but don't be mad at her. It was my idea. I wanted you to have a bit of lunch and we knew you wouldn't stop to eat any other way. Macara is in Vale now."

Cameron blinked. If he was debating whether to be angry at them for lying or grateful for Holly's concern, he decided on ignoring emotions altogether. Instead, he grabbed his coat and said, "At the Redwood?"

"Not this time. Roland is holding the council meeting at his home. Food and drinks not provided, despite Sal's protests." Holly's preoccupation with food provoked a quibble between her and Barnaby.

"Cameron is not interested in whether a feast's involved."

"I'm just explaining why I had him come here first."

"He doesn't need to know—"

The ding of the door interrupted their spat. "Thank you both." Cameron said, then he left Gooseberry's.

Or, he tried to.

Outside, he squinted at the path off Greenfield road that led up Vale Mountain. It was interesting to see Mr. Everly's car going up the mountainside. The only time he went up that way was when he was surveying Fairfield Castle for renovations, but why today of all days would he have reason to travel there?

Cameron's mind went to a strange, terrible place. He stepped back into Gooseberry's. Both Barnaby and Holly looked up, Barnaby with a turkey slice from his sandwich still hanging from his mouth.

"What is it, dear?" Holly asked.

"What do we know about the Everly family?"

Holly and Barnaby looked at each other.

"Well, you know Jane and Alden," Holly began.

Cameron waved a hand, wiping the idea away, "No, not Jane or Alden or Mrs. Everly. What do we know of Mr. Everly's family? The ones that came from England." Cameron's voice lowered as he sat back in the booth.

Barnaby, having chewed and swallowed the turkey slice, said, "Nothing, really. Some big deal from London. Wait, you're not saying that...."

Holly shook her head, "He isn't the right age. And you can forget the idea that Alden or Jane is going to betray Moss Hill. Miss Morgan herself raised those kids, and I've come to know Jane very well this past year. I wouldn't even think she's capable of something like that."

"The prophecy didn't say anything about ages. It only said, 'great-grandson.' Who knows how old the original druid or his descendants were when they each had children?"

"Even so, Mr. Everly is not a druid. Jane and Alden are druids only on their mothers' side," Barnaby said.

"What if the MacAirts are the druids who are in league with Maeb?" Cameron asked.

"Family lines are inherited through the father, so the prophecy wouldn't apply to Mrs. Everly or her children," Barnaby said.

Holly gave him a side-eye, saying, "Times have changed a bit, love. Nothing wrong with passing a prophecy onto a daughter. Not that I'm saying that's what happened."

Barnaby had enough sense to stuff the rest of his sandwich into his mouth instead of responding. Cameron ran his fingers through his hair. He was no closer to an answer, and the speculation would only drive him mad. He stood, heading for the door once again.

Holly called out as he left, "If you're really worried about this rumored prophecy, bring it up with the council. Someone there might provide an answer for you."

Chapter 8

Out of Deadlock

It was strange knowing she was being watched. Carissa felt Maeb's eyes on her, so she fought the temptation to run. Maeb would only catch her. Maybe she'd decide Carissa was too much trouble to deal with half-alive and send her into the World Beyond. She was wasn't ready for that. And Carissa couldn't move on until she knew Maeb's plan and figured out how to save Moss Hill from her.

The snow crunched beneath their her and Alden's feet. With his hands in his pockets and his shoulders scrunched up against the wind, Alden looked like an ordinary twenty-something. Gothic, maybe, and pale, but just a man strolling through the woods on a snowy afternoon.

Only these woods would freeze a living body in seconds.

Cold as she was, Alden could offer her no warmth. Even if she were willing to let him touch her, he was an ankou. A grim reaper could only be cold as death. That didn't mean they had to be cold-hearted. But Alden had been pretending, an imposter, a liar. His heart may well have been frozen.

"I know you hate me right now." He chanced a glance at Carissa.

She didn't look back. In the corner of her eye, Carissa saw Alden's lips fall, disappointed. He returned his gaze to the woods ahead.

"So? What is your story?" Carissa tried to be unfeeling in her tone, but couldn't be icy with Alden. There was still too much hope in her heart that he was the man she thought he'd been. He was Cameron's friend and hers, she'd thought. For that reason, she wanted to listen.

Alden took a deep breath. "I was in college when I got the diagnosis: pneumonia. My father was visiting at the time but my prognosis was good, and he left to attend to business he he'd come to England to settle. I don't think he, or I, realized I was so close to death. Perhaps if I had been in Moss Hill, Miss Morgan would have caught it. Even my mother might have tried to save me, though she isn't a practicing druid. My own powers were weakened from the illness.

"At first I just felt drained, then unable to cast any spells. Then I struggled to walk, then to breathe. By the time my father returned to discover I was dying, it was too late to send for help.

"In that time, I slept more often than I was awake. I dreamed dreams of these woods, this chill, this wind. Then I'd awaken, relieved that I'd been dreaming. Soon, reality blended with dreams and I lost my sense of either. Until one night, when I found myself here.

"I kept walking, like we are now, through this endless forest. And I kept waiting to wake up, but I couldn't. There was no cabin here then, just woods. Then I came upon a house. I think in the real world it was Tabitha's at the time. Only it wasn't Tabitha I met there but another woman."

"Maeb?" Carissa asked.

Alden nodded. "I didn't know who she was at the time, only that she said she could show me a way out—if I were willing to help her one day."

"With what?" Carissa asked.

"She said, 'Only a small matter of helping another person, just like yourself, as I am helping you now.'

"It seemed like kindness. And I was desperate, so I didn't question it. I said, 'Yes.'"

Alden stopped walking. He held a hand up, took a breath, dropped it, and raised it again. The air shimmered. Like a mirage in a desert, a path appeared.

Alden faced Carissa. "This is the path she showed me. It leads to the World Beyond."

"Maeb tricked you," Carissa said. "You were hanging onto life, and she led you to your death."

"It's where I'm supposed to lead you now," Alden took a step closer.

Carissa stiffened. "You don't have to do this. I promise we can save you."

"I made a promise, too," he said.

"Alden, don't do this. This is not who you are."

"I know it's not. I'm sorry," Alden said.

He took another step. Carissa readied her magic again. But Alden didn't pull her toward the path or thrust her into it. He put a hand on her face, gently, tenderly. The look in his eyes captivated her. He pulled her close…and kissed her.

His touch was tender, like a snowflake fallen on her lips. Tentative, tame as it was, it sent a shiver through her. She felt emotions mixing and swirling in her core. How could Alden kiss her? Didn't he know that was for Cameron alone? Yet, there was a rush from her heart through her entire body, like her elf-light surging.

It felt like magic.

Carissa realized then that it had been more than a kiss. Alden had given her some of his magic, the transfer disguised as a loving gesture. She could feel it coursing through her veins.

Alden's lips moved from her mouth to her ear as he whispered, "Run."

Then, he let go. Almost immediately, Cari heard the banshee-like cry of Maeb, and the wind picked up. Alden's hands flew to the air, creating a protective barrier.

Carissa caught a glimpse of black clouds surrounding Alden. She wasn't sure if it was Maeb's Tuatha de Danann magic or Alden's ankou powers, but she couldn't help. He was risking his afterlife for her. The best way to save him now was to get back to Moss Hill. There, she'd work with the others to rescue him from Maeb's grasp.

She promised herself this.

* * *

"WHAT IS IT you expect of us, Dorian?" Roland asked.

Head Elf Roland did not understand Christmas, except that his son-in-law, the elf-bard, artist, and architect, Fenigar, celebrated it. And his daughter had come to love it. So, it was a surprising sight to see garland hanging over the frosted windows, stockings hung above the green light of a faerie fire, and an Evergreen decorated with faerie dust and candles.

The elven council sat around the room, which seemed designed for a cozy conference with pillow-topped benches carved into the walls and the sofa and sofa chairs against the wall near the fireplace. The furniture, thus arranged in a full circle, conversation was easy.

Cameron, who had arrived late, heard Roland's question as he handed Sal, Roland's irreplaceable manservant, his coat. Sal never went without a smile, except that afternoon. His grave expression deepened as Cameron asked what had been said in the council so far.

"Roland is in a mood. He's had more than one piece of bad news today."

"He's heard about Maeb?"

"Mistress Jane arrived twenty minutes ago to inform the council. But it's worse than that."

"What is it?"

Sal set Cameron's coat on the coatrack by the door and walked just near enough for them to see into the living room. The councilmembers looked stern. Raz stood in the center of the circle with his head held high and a look of indignation in his eyes. It was clear he was defending himself from some accusation. Cameron looked at Sal, shocked and questioning.

Sal ducked back into the foyer, whispering, "Mayor Reg brought Raz here to address the council. Raz admitted to using the Talisman of Tethra before but he insists it was only to help our people. He's volunteering now to use his magic to save Carissa."

Cameron couldn't help but smile. "He can save her? I'm sorry I ever doubted him. Carissa said that Rhys Dwfen magic is strong—if it's strong enough to undo the tonic and remove the talisman, that's terrific news!"

Sal held a hand up, whispering, "Please, lower your voice. I didn't mean to raise your hopes like that. I'm sorry." He waved for Cameron to follow him into the kitchen, where he had prepared cider for the elves and other guests. As he poured, he explained, "Rhys Dwfen magic is too powerful. We're not supposed to use it—not our deep magic, just the basics."

"Why? Is Raz dangerous? Or does Roland fear his magic?"

"Dangerous? No. And why would anyone fear Raz or any of the Rhys Dwfen? You've known me all your life. You'd never fear me, would you?"

Cameron might have been quicker to answer "no" had Sal not been holding the cheese-knife up at just the wrong moment. But the answer was no. No one feared Sal or Raz or even Fudge, though the Everly's butler wasn't nearly as kind as the other two Rhys Dwfen on the island.

"You know I only have good feelings toward you, Sal. But I don't understand. Why isn't Roland letting Raz use his magic on Carissa?"

"We have magic that can upset the balance of things. That's why we seal our magic with our names. Once our true name is spoken, our deep magic awakens, and even we can't always control it. We don't always know how much to use and how it will affect the world around us. And this is exactly the kind of situation that can upset that balance. If Raz brings back Cari, he could bring back Maeb. She can attach her spirit to a half-dead person. She might even possess Cari's body. And if she were to attack Raz while using his magic...." Sal shuddered.

"It would be like an explosion, wouldn't it?"

"That or worse. She could steal his magic, too. Then, there would be no stopping her."

"Stealing magic, is that possible?"

"It's an old spell. It's forbidden now, but what would that mean to Maeb? She'd steal his magic in a heartbeat, and not just some of it—all of it until he has none left to stay alive."

Realization spread over Cameron's face. "This could have been her plan all along."

Sal's eyes teared. "Or she just wanted Cari dead, and this is a happy coincidence." He sobbed.

"Oh, Sal," Cameron said, eyes growing moist.

Sal put down the cheese knife. "I love her, too, you know. I watched her grow up and I know I'm not really family, but—" He sobbed.

Cameron pulled him into a hug. "You are family. And what's more, you've given me an idea. Don't worry, we'll save her. I think I just figured out how."

Chapter 9

Engaged in Conspiracy

Every path opened to Carissa. The ankou magic was quickly draining, but it was enough to get her to the right course. She felt a primal pull guiding her toward Moss Hill.

She was going to make it.

If Maeb didn't catch her first. Carissa was growing weak and tired from the sheer excursion of her spirit. When the roads diverged, one path toward Moss Hill and the other to the fae town of Vale, the thought occurred to her that this might be a trap. Not that Alden would deliberately have set her up, but Maeb might expect her to head for the church. So, Carissa diverted to Vale.

Her parents or Roland or anyone might have magic enough to sense her. Weak though she was, she could gain someone's attention. They might be able to get her back to her body or, at the very least, protect her from Maeb.

As she neared the stone steps leading up to the village of Vale, Carissa felt the cold air of the Borderlands releasing its grip on her lungs. She could breathe normally again. The world was still, calm, with no harsh winds around her.

It wasn't so much warm as just…not cold. And the light became brighter, cheerier. There was still something wrong about it—something different from the living world. But it wasn't the same feeling as the Borderlands. The dreamlike quality was gone and it felt like she was waking up.

"Oh no," she said aloud.

She had to turn back. This wasn't Vale.

It was the World Beyond.

"Don't fret, you won't die here—well, not any deader than you already are," a voice said.

A short, old woman with gnarled hands stood before her. The dog of death by her side, the woman stroking its fur. The hood of a black cloak covered her so that Carissa could not recognize her…until she looked up.

"Miss Morgan?"

Her withered face was holding the same scowl she wore in life. She put a slender finger to her lips. Then she waved Carissa toward her. "Let's not talk here. Come with me."

Miss Morgan led Carissa down the road to a small home close to the house where her parents lived. The barguest, a gentler dog here than he seemed in the living world, moved in front of them, wagging its tail the whole way. It felt strange following the barguest; though, in Miss Morgan's care, the hound seemed more like a pet than an omen of death.

Near her parents', they turned down a path Carissa hadn't seen before to a home Carissa did not recognize. It was camouflaged in a mound so that no one would recognize it if seen.

Inside, the furnishings were quaint. There was a table, some knotty wood chairs, a couch built into a wall with a large window behind it, though the window served no function since the outside was all moss and dirt. And there were shelves upon shelves with books and scrolls and all sorts of artifacts that looked very rare and ancient: gold statues, jewel encrusted knives, mirrors and stones Carissa suspected contained magic. Was Maeb in a vessel like this?

"No, this home doesn't exist in Moss Hill. It's from my memories. Everything here is created by mind and memory.

And those are powerfully magical, so please do not touch anything."

Carissa opened her mouth, horrified. "You can hear my thoughts?"

Miss Morgan rolled her eyes. "No, but you were staring loudly enough—at both the outside and inside of the house."

"Sorry, but it's all so strange. Like this window." Carissa pointed and saw smoke coming from the chimney of her parents' home. "My parents! Maybe if I could contact—"

"That's not your parents faerie fire you're seeing. You can't see anything of the living world, except through that enchanted glass you have in your pocket. And that's frowned upon here. It's healthy to keep connections to the living, but not to spy on them. I believe that's called haunting."

"But if I can't see my parents, who has lit a fire in their home?"

"Your grandfather."

"My grandfather is here?"

"He splits his time between Vale and Moss Hill. He goes everywhere around the towns—still thinks of himself as mayor, it seems. Before you ask: No. You cannot see him. He is dead, you are not."

"I'm talking to you," Carissa said.

"Yes, well, that's different. There's no emotion there, except for a little animosity between you and me and your poorly made tonics."

"They were not—" She stopped herself.

Miss Morgan had died from one of her tonics. Though it had been poisoned by someone else, she supposed Miss Morgan had a right to the last word there. She took a different approach. "So, you're saying I can't talk to my grandfather because it's too emotional?"

"You'll be all snotted up with tears and I do not want to see that. More importantly, you have to get back to the living world."

"I understand. I should return to the Borderlands before I get stuck here."

"You think the Borderlands and this are two different places?"

"This is the World Beyond, isn't it?"

Miss Morgan shook her head. "Your understanding is just like everyone else's. Thinking that the towns and cities are the World Beyond and the places barren of people are the Borderlands, as if they're two separate realms."

"Aren't they?"

Miss Morgan opened the drapes on the window, enchanting it to show Carissa the Borderlands and the homes in Moss Hill and Vale, here in the World Beyond. Carissa could see the familiar places and people who had passed, looking just as they had in life.

Miss Morgan explained, "You see the forest as a borderland because it's not what you think of as home. You aren't connected to it in a meaningful way and living there for eternity would feel like being unsettled. But in the towns like Moss Hill and Vale are the people you know and love and with whom you can spend forever. So, this becomes the World Beyond, a town where you can settle along with all those who came before you, waiting to welcome those who will come after you."

"But I'm half alive. So is Maeb, and the Borderlands-"

"Yes, yes, I know. How do I explain? When you're half alive, you are lost, neither connected to the living nor to the dead. The best way for your mind to process that is to put you in a place that isn't connected to anything—like the forest of Vale."

"Then, Maeb should be able to pass into the World Beyond—"

"You mean she could accept that she's dead? Yes. Maeb could let go of her links to the living."

"So, she isn't lying, then, about being half alive?"

"No, she is connected to both worlds or, I, along with all the seelie fae here, would have taken care of her already."

"Is that possible? To fight her from this side?"

"We've imprisoned her in the forest. While she's half-living, the only power we have over her is to keep her away from us."

"But she had the magic to guide Alden here."

"She did what?"

"She used her magic to open a portal to the World Beyond from the Borderlands. At least that's how Alden understood it."

"As ankou, he should know better. The Borderlands and the World Beyond—"

"—are the same. I understand that now. Maybe he was trying to keep it simple for me. But, he wasn't ankou at the time. He was dying and he couldn't find his way here without her help."

"You mean he couldn't let go of his body without her help. She influenced his mind to give up. See, Carissa, this is a realm of mind and spirit. Spirits don't need houses but minds do. Minds need sense and order and comfort."

"And love?" Carissa asked.

"Love is what the spirit needs. It's more powerful than any illusion needed for the mind. That's why it's dangerous to see anything or anyone here with whom you have a connection—it might make you forget your connection to the living world."

Carissa thought of her ties to the living. She loved her home, Nan, her parents, her friends, her apothecary shop, and, most of all, Cameron. Today was supposed to be the beginning of a whole new life with him. Soon they'd have a home together and build a family. "Nothing can make me forget that."

"Good. It's important not to linger here too long or your magic will run out and your connection to your body will die. And we'll be no closer to killing Maeb." Miss Morgan walked to the shelves and began rummaging through them.

"I don't want to kill anyone, not even her." Carissa recalled the accusation about her killing Niall Shae, and she shuddered.

"She's already dead. She just won't accept it. Ah, here it is." Miss Morgan took out a photo album and flipped through it. When she found what she was looking for, she took it from the page and handed it to Carissa.

"I thought we couldn't take stuff with us into the afterlife?"

"It's not 'stuff' from the living world. We can create things here with our own minds. This particular one comes from your grandfather's mind. I knew it would be important one day, so I had him make a duplicate for me."

Carissa looked at the photo: a drawing of four men and one woman standing outside Moss Hill City Hall: her grandfather, an elf, a sidhe, a human, and the woman was possibly a tylwyth teg changeling, but it was hard to tell if her skin was green in the graphite sketch.

"Who were they?"

"Are. They are the founders of Moss Hill and Vale. They may be gone from your perspective, but I had tea with Saoirse the other day."

"That's the woman in the photo?"

"Yes, but never mind her. It's this man I have to warn you about." Miss Morgan pointed to the human: a man with a square jaw, a sharp nose, and a mustache. His smile did not extend to his eyes, which were piercing, even in sketch form.

"Who is he?"

"Paden Finlay. He was a naval captain who discovered the island of Rhys Deep in his youth and proved himself to be loyal to the fae in time. In recent years, your grandfather has come to suspect that he may have been loyal to the followers of Maeb."

"What made him think that?"

"More and more unseelie have come to Moss Hill recently."

"I know. I think we've driven most of them away, though."

"Perhaps you have on your side of the great divide."

Carissa nearly dropped the sketch, "You mean that the unseelie in the World Beyond are 'coming' here?"

"Being drawn here or brought here."

"How?"

"The only thing we can glean from those we've captured is that they believe the great-grandson of Paden Finlay will restore Maeb to life."

"He's the one Belkin was talking about. I saw it through the mirror. He's in Moss Hill?"

"That's what I hope you can find out on your side. But you have to hurry. Your magic is draining. I can see it in your face."

"I'm not sure I'm strong enough to make it back to Moss Hill."

"Get to Tabitha. She can help."

"I thought you said we couldn't communicate with the living?"

"Her portals. The changeling portals work in every world. Use it to get to the one closest to your body. She can't harm you once you're back inside, she can't touch you."

To do that, she had to know where her body had been taken. Perhaps it was at home, where Nan was watching over her. Perhaps they'd left her at the church or taken her to Macara's to be under her care. The only way to know for sure was to use the shard of glass to see what was happening in the living world.

* * *

WHEN CAMERON ENTERED the discussion, it had turned into a heated argument about how to handle Maeb. Carissa, though she'd been the original topic of the emergency council meeting, was lost in the fray.

Dorian tried in vain to bring the discussion back to her. "My daughter is vying for her life—"

"With an enemy more treacherous than Moss Hill has ever faced," an elf interrupted.

Another added, "The Sidhe Council must be informed."

61

Jane said, "Varick took the news to them as I brought it to you."

"Well done and we thank you for that," a third elf said, adding, "But now that it is in sidhe hands—"

More passionately than Cameron had ever heard him, Dorian said, "Sidhe hands have made our hands idle. Too long and on far too many issues we have deferred and delegated decisions we ought to be making together for them to make alone. An elf's life is in the balance."

"Half-elf," someone muttered.

Dorian's eyes might have burned the wooden bench on which the mutterer had been seated if he'd known which elf had spoken.

Cameron stepped onto the wood floor of the living room, finally drawing the elves' attention onto him.

"Dorian's right. A half-elf, part-human, and part *Tuatha de Danann* is dying." He looked one of the elves in the eye, presumably the one who had spoken. The elf looked down and shifted in his seat. Cameron continued, "But, Dorian, no council is going to save her. Raz, it was brave of you to volunteer and, Reg, thank you for bringing him here. Jane, you were right to warn us all about Maeb and Varick was right to inform the sidhe, but these noble elves are also right. The sidhe won't decide what we're going to do. Roland, sir, I do hold high regard for this council and your position but, with all due respect, how we save Carissa isn't a choice for this council, either."

"You have a solution?" Roland asked.

Cameron nodded. "We gather the necessary magic into a single tonic and use that to break Carissa's spell."

"Stealing magic is against the law," an elf said.

"Not stealing, volunteering," Cameron said.

"Who would volunteer to give their magic? Even Raz cannot say yes to that. Once his deep magic is awakened—he can't transfer it safely," another elf said.

"Mossies stick together. All Mossies have magic—even the humans who don't think they do. We all have fae blood somewhere in our ancestry."

"But no Mossie is powerful enough to break the spell on Cari's talisman," Jane said.

"No single Mossie," Reg said with a smile. "That's brilliant. If enough Mossies were to combine their power, we'd have enough to heal Carissa and the talisman could safely be removed."

"Even if the councils both agree to break the ancient laws and allow a transfer of magic, we still can't use it as long as Cari's soul is lost in the Borderlands. We will have no way of knowing if it is Carissa's soul or Maeb's that returned."

"Wouldn't Alden know if it's Carissa or Maeb's?" Reg asked.

"Alden has been gone a long time. He may be in trouble," Jane said softly.

"Someone planned this. And whoever it was may have set this whole situation up as a trap. Or else why hasn't she made it out of the woods? And why hasn't Alden rescued her?" an elf asked.

The room went still so that only the snowfall outside reminded them that time was passing quickly.

"Someone has to go to the World Beyond," Macara said. Startling Cameron. He had no idea she was in the room, but there she was by the tree. Her sister, Raven, sat on the bench beside her.

"Yes, someone strong enough to face the Borderlands," Raven added.

Jane raised a hand. "I'll go. He's my brother, so I think it should be me."

"No," Macara said, perhaps out of a somewhat motherly concern or perhaps for a deeper reason.

"It has to be me," Cameron said.

"Err, Cam," Reg said with a wincing smile. "I don't mean to point out any shortcomings, but you don't exactly have any magic."

A soft chuckle broke from Raven's pursed lips. Smiling at Cameron, she said, "They don't give you enough credit, these elves. You humans are smart. You studied the ancient magic, didn't you?"

"The ancient magic? What do you mean?" Roland asked.

"The Mossies, the town, even the Borderlands—all these fae around and it took a human to figure out how it all works."

Reg asked, "How what works? What did he figure out?"

Raven tapped the side of her nose, "Don't explain."

"It has to be you. But are you strong enough?" Macara asked.

Cameron said, "For Carissa, I will always be strong enough to do what is needed of me."

Chapter 10

On the Rocks

Carissa could sense Maeb even before she left Vale. She stayed close to the moss-covered boulders until there were no more in sight. Looking in all directions, she traveled cautiously between redwoods. Maeb could surely sense her (she was sensing Maeb), but as long as she stayed unseen, she would not be caught. She hoped.

By the time Tabitha's cottage came into view, so did Maeb. Carissa ducked behind the root of a massive redwood. Thankfully, she hadn't chosen a flowy wedding dress with a train too large to hide. She was able to scrunch down and peek above the root to study Maeb.

She was standing beside the picket fence, but not by the portal. Carissa judged the distance. She might be able to make it, but not without being seen. Maeb was facing her and the portal. She'd see Carissa if she tried to dash for it, and, with Alden's magic all but gone, she couldn't protect herself from an attack.

Alden was nowhere in sight, leaving Carissa to wonder what had happened to him in his confrontation with Maeb. She couldn't have destroyed Alden but might have hurt him badly. She might be keeping him prisoner. Or was she conspiring with him?

She was talking with someone whom Carissa couldn't see. She wasn't sure if Alden had the power not to manifest himself, if there was some other invisible person beside her, or if Maeb was certifiably insane.

"I will find her. You do your part. Or are you afraid?"

Silence, then.

"You have nothing to worry about. Macara and Raven have their limits. There's no better place for our revolution than Moss Hill. Don't forget that it was a Tuatha de Danann who paved the way for my resurrection. Just do what I ask, and you and your family will have the whole island in your control."

Carissa gasped. She clamped her hand over her mouth, then ducked behind the tree root, praying Maeb hadn't heard her. Once her heart calmed, she gathered her courage to look again.

Maeb had a hand to her forehead. "Problems. That's all you bring to me," she was saying.

Carissa breathed a silent sigh of relief. Maeb hadn't noticed her. But, it was clear to her now that the person to whom Maeb was speaking was the conspirator in the living world. Carissa wasn't the only one with that ability. She took out the shard of glass and whispered into it, "Tabitha."

The glass showed Tabitha in her kitchen, yelping loudly. Tabitha raised the pan, flipping the contents of her lunch onto the floor. She stepped right in the mess of green beans and mushrooms as she held the pan like a weapon.

"Who's there?" she yelled.

At the same time, Maeb said, "Well, get out of there then. Don't let her see you."

"Tabitha, you need to stop yelling. It's me." Carissa said. She waved into the glass.

Carissa's image was waving from a mirrored kitchen cabinet.

Tabitha nearly pressed her nose against it. "Carissa? Is that you? Oh, thank goodness you're alive! I was so worried."

"Tabitha, you need to look outside, there's someone by your portal. I think they're conspiring with Maeb."

"Okay," Tabitha nodded.

"Don't let them see you," Carissa added. She braved another look at Maeb and ducked back immediately.

Maeb surveyed the forest, her eyes scanning left and right. Then, she spoke loudly. "I know you're there. I can feel you. Why are you hiding? I wouldn't harm my own flesh and blood, Carissa. Come home."

Tabitha's voice resounded through the glass. "I didn't see anyone. Who am I looking for? Carissa? Cari?"

Carissa turned the mirror down, to muffle the sound. "Shh. I'm not safe. Maeb is nearby."

"Maeb?" Tabitha nearly shouted.

She fled from the mirror. "Tabitha?" Carissa whispered.

Whatever she'd done, where ever she'd gone, Maeb must have felt it because she cursed, "Blasted changeling! I'm not your enemy, Cari. You cannot stay out here forever. And you cannot get back to Moss Hill without help—no one in the living world will see you. Sooner or later, you'll come back to me," her voice trailed off as if she were walking further and further away. But Carissa suspected it was a trap. She waited a long while before risking another peek from her hiding spot. When she finally did look, Tabitha's cottage was gone. And so was the portal.

She looked back in the mirror, "Tabitha? Tabitha!"

Tabitha reappeared in the mirror, beaming.

Carissa asked, "What did you do?"

"Bonded my home to Moss Hill, so it wouldn't be visible in the World Beyond. Of course, it won't be visible in Vale, either." She put a hand to her chin, "I'm going to need to undo the spell eventually."

Carissa couldn't even fathom that kind of magic. Changeling magic worked so differently from other fae powers that it confused her half the time and astounded her the other half. But she could puzzle about that later. "You need to undo the spell now. I need that portal to get back to town."

"Oh, alright, hold on."

She disappeared again. A few seconds later, the cottage and portal came back into sight. Tabitha reappeared in the mirror. "Can you see it again?"

"I can, thank you."

"Be honest, do you like it? I'm having it remodeled to open Tabitha's Vale Heights Bed and Breakfast. What do you think? Cari?"

Carissa had to move out of the mirror's sight to roll her eyes. Trust Tabitha never to know the appropriate time or place for conversation. Moving back into frame, she said, "It's lovely. I have to go, Tabitha, thanks again."

"Oh, no problem. I have to go, too. There's someone at the door."

Carissa's eyes shot wide, "Wait! Don't answer it, yet."

But the mirror faded, and her attempt to recontact Tabitha failed. Whoever was Maeb's accomplice, they could very well be ensnaring Tabitha into a trap this very moment. And Carissa was helpless to stop them. She had to get back to the living world, the sooner the better.

* * *

GOOSEBUMPS RAISED ON Cameron's arms. He shivered before lowering himself onto the chaise beside Carissa. The light was fading outside the church, and the small room felt dreary in candlelight. Dorian draped his arms around his wife. He watched as Macara and Holly prepared the spell that would send Cameron to the borderland between life and death. Raven stood by the window as if watching the snow was more important, essentially killing Cameron, temporarily.

The tonic Holly had brewed was bitter, and he wanted to spit it out but drank anyway. Chaos sipped it as well while making a sour face. Cameron and Chaos exchanged fearful glances before she curled into a ball on the chaise beside his head. Holly's reassurances did little to ease the situation.

"You're sure this will work?" Cameron asked, lying flat and staring up at the ceiling.

Tonics and Turning Points

"If you mean 'will it take you to the Borderlands between life and death?' then yes."

"And bring us back? Right? You didn't say 'and bring you back.'"

"As long as you keep your connection with Macara, you'll be fine," Raven said, still not looking away from the window.

"Relax," Macara said. "You have nothing to worry about. All you have to do is find Carissa, make sure that it is her that returns to her body. She may need you to make the final leap back into this world."

Cameron nodded. "I have no doubt my connection to her will work."

The chiming sound of Chaos's wings drew their attention and she signed something only Raven could understand. "Yes, yes, I'm sure your connection is strong, too."

Hiya and Cynth went to the chaise beside Cameron.

"Where do you think you're going?" Holly asked.

"Oh let them, Maeb won't consider them targets," Raven said.

Macara lifted her arms and began to chant. Cameron took Carissa's hand. Then he closed his eyes and tried to listen. The words were ancient and ominous. They sent a chill through Cameron's ears to the core of his heart. The cold clutched at his insides and would not let him breathe. His head spun until the chanting turned into the howling of wind whistling in his ears.

He was standing now, though he couldn't open his eyes to see where he and the sprites had traveled. What was worse, he couldn't breathe. He sucked in air, coughing and collapsing to his knees. He opened his eyes. Cameron and Chaos found themselves in the churchyard under a dimly lit sky that made everything seem unreal.

Chaos, Hiya, and Cynth floated above him, seeming to take the cold better than he was. Chaos sprinkled faerie dust over Cameron like a blanket. His reddening cheeks and nose returned to their natural color. He stood upright and broad-shouldered at his full height.

"Thanks," he said. "Any idea where Alden and Carissa are?"

Chaos closed her eyes. After a few seconds of deep concentration, she opened them and nodded. She thrust her palm open and faerie dust flew to the ground ahead of her.

"A path, great idea, but I think it's better if you just lead the way. We shouldn't leave a path for anyone to track us."

He walked as he talked, and with each step he took forward, the dust on the ground faded. "Well, I guess that takes care of that."

Chaos put her petite hand on Cameron's cheek. His eyebrows furled but, even before he could ask what was wrong, she zipped off, leaving a trail of faerie dust for him to follow.

"Chaos!" he whispered loudly. He wouldn't yell in this place; it was too full of the unknown.

Hiya and Cynth looked at each other and shrugged. They waved at Cameron and then raced ahead, too. Their fluttering wings left a cloud of faerie dust.

Batting their magic away, he threw up his hands. "All right. I get it. You're literally leaving me in your dust. I can do this without you, thanks very much."

He followed the trail past the churchyard and onto Greenfield. Up the road to Vale, he came across a dog with glowing red eyes, mangy fur, and large teeth. The barguest stared him down.

Cameron froze.

"You must be the Dog of Death." With considerable bravery, Cameron added, "I know your passphrase. *Ní fhaigheann laochra choíche bás*: The brave never die. I am brave enough and strong enough to enter these woods. Let me pass."

The barguest regarded him with a cocked head and an intimidating stare. When Cameron did not back down, the dog turned and trotted up the hill, leading him forward.

Tonics and Turning Points

Cameron breathed a sigh of relief and traveled up the mountain.

"I'm coming, Carissa, just hold on."

Chapter 11

Vow to Live

Before Carissa felt safe enough to jump through the portal, she took one last look through the glass. The mirror wouldn't show her the woods but would show her the church. So, she watched as Cameron went under. Then, she willed the mirror to show the churchyard in the Borderlands, and she watched through the windows over every store and bakery as Cameron walked down the road to Vale. But she was at the portal and could will herself through to the corner of Greenfield and Gorse. There was no need for him to come all the way. She had to meet him before he made it up the path.

There was only one way to do that. She gathered the fabric of her dress in one hand, took a deep breath, and stood. She launched herself over the tree root and ran. Dirt and moss flew as she darted the last stretch of the clearing to the portal. In a second of hesitation, it dawned on Carissa that she'd never traveled through one of Tabitha's portals before.

She thought of her destination at the portal on Greenfield Road and plunged herself, face first, into the portal. The sensation was odd. It felt like going down a waterslide and falling untethered through the air at the same time. She felt carried by a wind that might let go of her at any moment.

That was the least of her worries as she felt a hand grasp her wrist and pull. She screamed and felt herself tumbling forward. She fell through the other side of the portal rolling thrice until landing with a thud on the ground. Her captor landed beside her, still holding her wrist.

"Let go of me!" Carissa struggled to wrench her hand away from none other than Maeb herself.

"You didn't think I was going to let you go so easily, did you?" she taunted. And she let go of Carissa's hand but Carissa wasn't getting away.

Maeb closed her eyes. She took a breath in and out as if refreshing her strength. When Maeb's eyes opened, behind Carissa stood Fairfield Castle, just as Mrs. O'Brien had restored it.

"Look at it. Our battleground, Raven's and mine, when we were young."

Carissa kept silent, but inwardly she felt her gut twisting. There was no way she could imagine Raven siding with Maeb, not in any past, or now.

"We ruled all the way from Connaught to Hy Brasil. We would have had that, too, if all had gone to plan." Maeb turned toward Carissa, "You and I still can. With this castle as our base and Moss Hill as our first conquest, we would have druids and fae and humans under our command—as is the natural order."

Carissa said, "The natural order is equality, friendship, and the harmony that has been created here in Moss Hill. Can't you see what a beautiful world we've built?"

Maeb scoffed, "Beautiful world? Where this castle becomes a tourist attraction for people who know nothing of its true history?"

A voice came from near the castle gate. "I know the history. I've studied all of it."

Cameron emerged from the shadowed archway of the castle gate. He wasn't alone, the Black Dog of Death walked beside him as it had stood beside Miss Morgan: dutifully. Carissa attempted to move toward him, but Maeb held her palm up straight and shot out a grey cloud of Tuatha de Danann magic. It wrapped around her wrists and shoulders, holding her back.

"Don't struggle against it." Cameron surprised her with his calmly stated command.

Maeb cackled, "You did choose a smart one! Quite right, don't struggle, dear girl."

Carissa stopped trying to pry herself loose. The grey magic rose to her neck, and she looked at Cameron with wide eyes. What was he doing? She had to keep moving. There was no way to stay still without being enveloped by Maeb. Did Cameron not realize the peril?

He put his hands out. "Cari, look at me. You don't need to struggle. You already have a stronger connection to me than you do her. All you have to do is focus on me."

"I can't," she croaked as Maeb's magic tightened around her throat.

He walked closer. "You can. All you need is to remember your connection to the living world—your connection to me."

"No," Maeb tightened her grip, "You don't have enough magic to get back to your body. You don't have the magic to fight me."

Cameron reached out, touched Carissa's fingertips, her wrists, her arms. Everywhere he touched her, Maeb's grey magic evaporated.

Carissa looked at Cameron, amazed.

"How is this possible?" Maeb looked down at her palms. She tried again to form a cloud around them, but as the mist breached her fingertips, it recoiled. Again and again, she tried and failed to reach them. Each time, the magic around Cameron and Carissa grew brighter as if they were surrounded by swirls of light. Maeb marveled, "No magic is this strong."

Cameron looked up at Maeb, but he wasn't speaking to her when he said, "Now."

The barguest leaped at Maeb. He gnashed his teeth at her, catching her in the forearm. Maeb wrestled the beast off and tried to hit him with her magic. The dog kept her occupied long enough for Cameron and Carissa to run to the portal.

This time they traveled to the destination Carissa had intended to go. Once inside the churchyard, Cameron pulled Carissa toward the doors of the church.

Tonics and Turning Points

"Wait. We have to go back. We have to save Alden," Carissa said.

"We can't. We need to get you back to your body."

"I'm stronger now. I can help him." She broke free of Cameron's grasp and took a step forward. But outside of his embrace, Carissa felt her energy drain. She gasped and stumbled. Cameron caught her by the waist.

"Something is wrong. You're weaker. We have to get you back to your body." Cameron scooped her into his arms.

"Maeb is coming." Carissa could see the cloud of gray coming closer. "I need magic to fight her." She tried to summon her magic.

"Stop. You can't use magic, Cari. It will drain you. Jane is bringing you a tonic with Mossie magic in it to save you, but you have to make it to your body first. You don't need magic here."

Still holding her, Cameron ran down Greenfield toward the church. The whole sky above them turned dark. The wind began to pick up.

Carissa shook her head. "I can't let Maeb get to us. I can't let her get a hold of my body."

Cameron, stopped running. "There has to be an easier way." He looked down the road and concentrated on the church. He closed his eyes.

"Cameron?" Carissa asked.

Cameron's eyes snapped open. "Have you noticed that this place feels like a dream? Miss Morgan said this is a realm of mind and spirit. Your grandfather had a theory that, like a dream, the World Beyond can overpower us, interact with us and make us helpless. But in dreams, the minute we realize we're dreaming we can control that world."

Just like that they were in the churchyard. Carissa clung to Cameron. She was still weak but felt energized by the awe she felt for him in that moment. She put a hand to his cheek. "I always knew you had magic in you."

A troubled look passed over Cameron's face. "Raven was right. It feels like magic and she wondered if I was strong enough to give it up." He got to the church door and pushed it open, saying, "I am. I want to live my life with you." He walked to the bride's room and laid her down on the chaise.

Carissa smiled, looking up at Cameron with pure joy. Then a surge of pain shot through her. Carissa's eyes teared, and her heart, though drained of magic, was overflowing with love.

"I don't think I can make it," she said.

"When we're in the living world again, Macara can help sustain you until Jane brings you the tonic. All you need to do is get back to your body."

"How?" she asked. Hot and cold shot through her skin and veins. She felt as though life itself was being ripped away from her.

Cameron held her hand and stroked her cheek, saying, "Just think of your connection to the living world—to me. Remember all the things you have to live for, that we have in store for us."

"Then give me a reminder," Carissa said.

She slipped her fingers on the back of Cameron's neck and pulled him to her. Alden had transferred his power to her in this way. In Cameron's case, perhaps his strength of will, his connection to the living world, his love for her, would give her enough strength to get home. And even if it didn't work, she needed to feel Cameron's lips against hers.

Rather than the icy-cold sensation she'd felt with Alden, Cameron's kiss warmed her inside and out. It was a more profound connection than magic alone, and it set afire every part of her being: mind, body, and soul.

Chapter 12

To Have and To Hold

C arissa and Cameron awoke, hand in hand, on the chaise in the bridal preparation room in the church. Carissa was immediately swept into her mother's arms. Macara broke her link with Cameron with a magical incantation while Holly helped the two of them stand.

It was disorienting to be back in a body. Carissa felt heavier, noticing the weight of her physical being for the first time. But as she stood, she noticed something else.

"My magic It's gone." Carissa put a hand over her chest, feeling the thud of her heartbeat but sensing no magic in her veins. She had only discovered her Tuatha de Danann magic recently, but her elf-light was a part of her. She'd never felt so empty.

She wanted to ask Cameron, Maren, or Nan if this is what it was like for them. Being human, they'd never known the sensation of light-magic coursing through them. It was a rhythm, a lightness of foot, and an energy that flowed through her and around her. It connected her to the natural world in ways she'd never fully appreciated. Without it, she felt disconnected...lost.

Cameron looked at Macara and Raven in turn.

Raven put her hands up. "You were convulsing. We had to take a chance."

Macara said, "We had to seal the talisman's power, which, in turn, sealed your magic, too. You have no magic right now, Carissa. I'm sorry."

"You said that would kill her!" Cameron cried.

Raven replied, "And if she were any other fae, she would be dead. But she is part human. That part is sustaining her now. With luck, it will be able to keep her alive long enough to save her."

"But, without my magic, won't the tonic still kill me?"

Holly explained, "All the magic in your body is locked. That includes what was in the spell that was enhancing the ingredients in the tonic. Without the tonic's magic, its ingredients are harmless. All we have to do is wait. Once the tonic is out of your body, you should be safe and we should, theoretically, be able to unlock your magic and remove the talisman."

"Raven, what did you mean her human half has to keep her alive long enough to save her? Is there a chance she'll die before the tonic can leave her system?" Cameron asked.

Macara answered, "No fae has ever lived without any magic. We don't know how long the human part of Carissa can keep the rest of her alive."

Carissa said, "I've never felt like this before. Even when I didn't know how to use it, I've always felt my magic in me. I feel strange without it."

"Feeling anything is good. It means you're still alive," Raven said.

The thought of her being alive made Carissa think of Alden, and how he had been less fortunate. "Alden is still out there, unprotected."

Raven waved a hand, "Chaos, Hiya and Cynth have gone to find him. He'll be fine."

"They're just sprites. They could be in danger, too."

Raven scoffed, offended. "You should know better than anyone the might sprites possess when pressed. Besides, Chaos is crafty. I have no doubt she can slip past Maeb and rescue Alden."

"But how will she find Alden? And, even if she does, if he's too weak, how will she bring him back? Chaos can't carry Alden the way Cameron carried me to the church. And what if Maeb does catch her? I know the power of the mind is important in the World Beyond, but Maeb has a powerful will of her own."

"Cameron can answer these questions. He's the one who figured it out." Raven said.

Cameron nodded. "There is a belief among humans that when you die, your loved ones surround you. I've always thought that's because those are the people with whom you have the strongest bonds. I can't explain Chaos's connection with Alden, but there's no disputing that it's there. She's been able to summon him from the beginning. So, she should be able to find Alden and, if she has as strong a bond as I think, she can pull him to the right place in the World Beyond or bring him home here. All he needs is her will to save him and his will to live."

"The human will," Raven said, "is often underestimated, especially by heartless souls like Maeb."

Macara said, "And love. I anchored Cameron to the living world, but it was his love for you and the future you'd share together that, ultimately, brought you back."

Carissa nodded. She understood it now, all except one thing. "So, Alden's strongest connection is with Chaos?"

Raven chuckled. "Quite the other way around. Chaos was smitten at first sight. We could have sent Jane. I think her sisterly connection may have been enough to bring Alden home, too. But, she's too valuable to Moss Hill as its protector. We couldn't risk her. Still, I honestly fear more for Maeb in a confrontation with Chaos than the other way around."

Carissa smiled at that or tried to. But she was too worried to picture a fight between Chaos and Maeb as anything but devastating. And she truly feared what Maeb might do too Hiya and Cynth.

"I have to go back. I have to rescue them."

Macara said, "I'm sorry, but no. You are the keeper of the gates between the Otherworld and the human world. The Tuatha de Danann gave you that responsibility and our duty is to protect you. The consecrated ground offers some security against spirits, but Maeb has many living souls who do her bidding. My home is the safest place for you now."

Carissa repeated, "Souls who do her bidding. She said something about that. She said there was a Tuatha de Danann on her side, or more than one? I'm not sure. She was talking to someone in the woods. Reassuring them that there were many unseelie on their side. And Maeb said it was a Tuatha de Danann who had helped her so that she had a way to come alive again."

Macara shot Raven a suspicious look. To that, Raven rolled her own eyes as if to say, *"Of course, it wasn't me."*

Carissa said, "There's more. I think Tabitha may be in danger."

* * *

CARISSA COULD NOT believe that she'd been forbidden to help the sprites, but was even more shocked when she was not allowed to check on Tabitha. She was feeling fine, albeit weaker without her magic. She could have at least made a car ride there, but Macara and Raven wouldn't hear it. They would check on Tabitha themselves, both of them. Then they'd look for Maeb's vessel. They had been giving each other the side-eye since hearing about the betrayal of a Tuatha de Danann.

Cameron wouldn't disobey their orders, or maybe he secretly agreed with them. He drove Carissa and Holly to Macara's home. To be on the safe side, he and Holly checked over the house to ensure it was secured, both physically and magically.

"The house is enchanted, and Jane will be over soon to stay with you." Cameron kissed Carissa and turned to leave, but she held him back.

"I don't need watching over. I want to help."

Tonics and Turning Points

"The best help you can give is to let yourself heal. I'll tell your parents in Vale that you are fine and I'm sure the councils will want an update on your progress."

So, she was confined to Macara's home with Holly cooking supper and Jane on the way to provide her further protection. So many people doting on her made Carissa feel like an invalid. What was worse was the feeling of helplessness.

She should be preparing against any further attacks from Maeb. She should be investigating Maeb's secret accomplice. She should be doing anything aside from sitting by the fireplace enjoying the scent of the four-course dinner Holly was cooking.

Holly wouldn't even let her exert herself in the kitchen because of her fragility. So Carissa sat, listening to Holly cutting vegetables, enjoying the aroma of the potato-garlic soup bubbling on the stove, and turning facts over in her mind to determine who could have been helping Maeb. Again and again, she came up short. There was no Mossie who would betray Moss Hill like that.

Mayor Belkin had been hiding books, that's true, but that was hardly enough to make him unseelie. And, aside from that, Carissa wasn't sure he could be a Finlay, since he was at least part fae if not fully a troll. He'd always been greedy and ambitious, though, and his opening up the island to tourism had allowed the unseelie to come to their shores. But, arguably, the unseelie would have come, anyway, and the influx of tourists had benefitted Moss Hill in other ways.

The idea of Reginald being related to the Finlay family was laughable. He cared about Moss Hill and he had been working with a Tuatha de Danann, MacLir. MacLir was a friend to Raven and Macara, and had appointed Alden as ankou for Moss Hill.

Alden had betrayed Carissa, but not of his own free will. He had risked his life for Carissa and would never bring Macara back from the dead. The thought of him having been a Finlay, plotting against her and Cameron this whole time, made her feel sick. A feeling that did not leave her until she heard Jane knocking on the door.

Holly rushed around the kitchen island, but Carissa held a hand out.

"It's Jane, I saw her from the window," she said, getting up from the couch by the fireplace.

When she opened the olive-green, wooden door, she was surprised to see Tabitha on the other side with Jane. Tabitha reached out and pulled Carissa into a hug. Carissa struggled to breathe with how tightly Tabitha was squeezing her.

"You're alive!" Tabitha said, rocking her back and forth in her embrace.

Jane, standing behind her, holding an umbrella and a tote bag, said, "I've brought you a change of clothes and the tonic of Mossie magic."

Holly shouted from the kitchen, "No tonic! Her magic is sealed and we can't risk unsealing it until the poison is out of her system. The Mossie magic is a last resort."

"Thanks, Jane," Carissa squeaked out, then she patted Tabitha's back, "Um…Tabitha? You can let go of me now."

"Oh." Tabitha released her. "Sorry."

Holly peeked her head out of the kitchen, "You're here, too? Goodness sakes, I'll call Macara on this celly contraption."

No one bothered to correct her to say that it was a cell phone.

"What are you doing here?" Carissa asked.

"Mr. Everly drove me up here, and then Jane said she was coming over here to babysit you."

"To sit with you," Jane's eyes widened, and she looked at Carissa apologetically.

Carissa smiled to show no offense had been taken.

"But why did Mr. Everly pick you up at all?"

Tabitha let herself in and sat on the couch. "He came to my house to talk about his expansion project. He said he'd invest in my bed and breakfast and double the size of my house for a share of the profit. He had the plans all drawn up, but then I said I wanted to see it because you can never be too careful in business, and little Otto Jr. needs a stable future.

"Otto Jr.?" Jane smiled. "Have you got a bun in the oven?"

Misunderstanding the idiom, Tabitha said, "Oh, no. He's more than a bun. I shaped him already, cute button nose and all, but you don't actually put a changeling in an oven. That would be dangerous. It's right into the faerie fire for seven hours, just enough time for the magic to bring him to life. But I haven't put him in yet. I'm waiting for just the right time."

Jane could not have looked more puzzled. But Tabitha had no idea that her description of childbirth was anything but ordinary. It would be too much to explain that crimble changelings were born out of clay and faerie fire. Tabitha was a natural-born changeling of a different type than her late husband, Otto Crimbal. Most would not understand that upon his death the clay-like mud out of which he'd been created was left over and, out of that, Tabitha had chosen to craft her and Otto's son. That was something best left to Tabitha to explain. Carissa tried to get the conversation back to more pressing matters.

"Why does Mr. Everly want to invest in your bed and breakfast?" What she really wanted to ask was, wasn't it strange that Mr. Everly was at her door seconds after Maeb's mystery conspirator. Still, with his daughter, Jane, right next to her, she couldn't point any fingers.

"My father sees Vale as an opportunity since they're opening up more to Mossie influence. The fae don't have stores and other buildings, and, since he can't have Fairfield castle, he needed somewhere else to invest."

"I thought ownership went to the MacAirts?" Carissa had thought that the deal was all but done.

Jane said, "Mrs. O'Brien is still fighting us for ownership. She wants it declared a historic site so that my father cannot turn it into an inn, as he wants to do. He took a walk with her in Fairfield today to try to persuade her to become a part owner/investor, so that it would be a win-win. She said she was convinced there was another project that the city council is more likely to favor," Jane said.

"What project?" Tabitha moved closer, intrigued.

"I'm afraid I don't know," Jane said.

Carissa sat silent. As long as the project wasn't the headquarters for Maeb's war campaign, it was fine with her. But she had to wonder whether it was Mr. Everly or Mrs. O'Brien who'd met Maeb in the woods. There was always the possibility of another person. Though, in her heart, Carissa couldn't think of any Mossie betraying their own town. She had to investigate further.

"Jane, after dinner could we go to your home for a while? I know Macara said to stay here, but you're still watching over me whether it's here or there. And a change of scenery might be nice."

Jane glanced over at Holly, who was still working away on dinner. "All right, sure. I'm sure my parents will be glad to see you."

Tabitha clapped her hands, "And you can see Mr. Everly's plans for Vale and Moss Hill."

"Perfect," Carissa said. "I want to know everything about it."

Chapter 13

Hearts and Souls

After dinner, the Everlys agreed to drive Tabitha home. Carissa worried for her safety, but with Mrs. Everly there, too, Tabitha would likely be safe. So she said nothing and stayed with Jane and Holly at the Everlys mansion. At the moment, the two of them were more focused on reopening the mirror from this side of the portals. Carissa watched as they tried to figure out how the magic worked.

"How did you do this, what did you call it, mirror magic?" Jane asked.

"I don't know. I put my hand on the glass and thought of who I wanted to contact. My magic did the rest."

Holly said, "Move aside. I've seen Macara do it before." Holly put her palm flat on the glass.

"Maybe it needs Tuatha de Danann magic?" Jane asked.

Holly scratched her head, "We'll have no luck with that. Cari's magic is locked under a spell, and Raven and Macara may be a few hours."

"Did they have any luck finding Maeb's vessel?" Carissa asked. They weren't looking for Tabitha anymore since she knew she was safe.

"They're still looking around town for a statue, or some historical item that might hold her soul. If they can find it and destroy it, we'll have nothing to worry about," Holly said.

"Nothing except that we can't find my brother." Jane placed both hands on the mirror and closed her eyes.

Carissa picked up Holly's cell phone, which she spotted sitting on the table. "Holly, can I use your phone?"

"My what?" Holly asked.

"Your celly contraption," Carissa clarified.

"Why?"

"I want to see if Cam is still in his meeting with the Elf and Sidhe Councils," she lied. "Please?"

"All right. Tell him to bring me back some mistletoe from Vale while he's there. The ones from Moss Hill are just not the same." Carissa held the device out and Holly pressed her thumb on the screen to unlock it.

Carissa grinned. She couldn't use magic, but who said humans had no magic of their own? She called Maren.

Maren answered on the first ring, "Holly?"

"It's Carissa."

"Cari? It's so good to hear your voice. I was just heading over to you now. Your nan and I packed some things for you. Do you prefer your green cardigan or your red sweater?"

"Forget that. I mean, thanks, either one is fine, but I borrowed some clothes from Jane, so there's no rush." She looked down at the pink cashmere sweater and matching pants, almost wishing Jane would tell her she could keep them. "Listen, can you ask Tilly to do a background check on someone for me? The man's name is Paden Finlay. Tell her to call me back on this number when she's done, will you?

"Paden Finlay. Got it. What else?"

"That's all. Oh, and could you grab some mistletoe from the Seelie Tree. I'll explain later."

"Okay, I'll pretend like both your requests make sense. I'll see you in a bit."

Carissa laughed softly, "Thanks, Maren. You're the best." She was better than she knew. Carissa didn't really suspect Reg, but if he was secretly a Finlay, Carissa had just asked her to gather incriminating information on her own boyfriend.

At the end of the phone call, Carissa realized that Holly's phone had Macara's number programmed into it. She smirked, thinking how strange it was for a fae and a Tuatha de Danann to have human technology. Carissa found Macara's contact information and put a video call through to Macara to see how she and Raven were faring. The two butted heads more often than not, and their discovery of a Tuatha de Danann ally had only strained the relationship further.

Macara answered with the phone upside down.

"Yes, oh, that's new." She turned the phone around, "What's wrong, are you all right?"

"Fine. Any luck finding Maeb's vessel tying her to the living world?"

"None yet. Where are you going?" Macara turned both ways on the cobblestone street corner before deciding to follow her sister. Carissa saw a brief glimpse of Raven holding a large brown paper.

"I'm following this map. Why?" Raven didn't look back.

"That map of Moss Hill is two centuries old. Things have moved—changed," Macara said.

"But that's exactly why the map is perfect." Raven stepped back in the picture. She stopped at the stone statue of a raven, one Carissa had once thought symbolized Raven herself.

She swirled back, pointing, "That's it."

"The raven?"

"No, and yes, both. Here. The inscription reads: *The Raven Prepares for War.*"

"No need to brag, dear sister. I know the statue honors you. Though, war is nothing to celebrate, in my opinion."

"When it's necessary, and it's won, it is. But that's not the point. Maeb said that her likeness is in Moss Hill, encasing a remnant of her spirit. But, what if it's not a bust of her or a part of her being. What if it's a likeness of her familiar?"

"What in the worlds is a familiar?" Macara asked.

"A witchy term for people who don't understand what we are—you know, the animal she's connected to?"

"Not sure that helps. She's a battle crow, same as you," Macara said.

"A crow hasn't been mine for centuries. Morrigan took that connection as hers. I took the raven. I don't know what animal Maeb used to send messages, if any, but all of us, I think, used crows at one point."

"So, we find a symbol of a crow," Macara reasoned.

"Is there a statue of a crow anywhere in Moss Hill?" Carissa asked.

Raven's nose and chin appeared on the screen. "No, but there are plenty of live ones. Perhaps she's not attached to an artifact, but to a living being or even a flock of birds."

"Our sisters' crows. I talk to them, too. They don't seem very unseelie to me," Macara said.

"Very? Why did you say it like that? Do you mean they seem 'a little' unseelie?" Raven asked.

"Cranky, that's all. You know how Morrigan was, they picked up her way of emoting." Alarm widened Macara's eyes. "Oh, sis, you don't think Morgan was the Tuatha de Danann who was on Maeb's side?"

"The unseelie killed her, remember? No, that would make no sense. And, furthermore, I don't think any Tuatha de Danann is on her side. I think she just said that to get us to stop trusting each other." The hurt in Raven's eyes was visible.

Carissa sensed that Macara lost a bit of trust in her sister after hearing that Maeb had a Tuatha de Danann accomplice. Her heart sank as she admitted to herself that she, too, had felt some doubt toward Raven. It wasn't just Raven's brusque personality, Maeb herself had said she'd been friends with Raven.

Tonics and Turning Points

The thought of Maeb reminded her why she'd called. *Maeb still has Alden. We're trying to see them in the looking glass, but—"*

"Cari, come quickly!" Jane's voice interrupted.

Raven said, "Oh, don't worry about that. Cameron's determined to save him. He'll be just fine."

"Cameron?" Carissa asked.

Macara said, "We sent Cameron and Varick back into the Borderlands at Cam's request."

Holly called out, "We've got Chaos in the mirror. And it looks like she's got herself some reinforcements."

Chapter 14

Dream of a Funeral

The most nerve-racking sight up to now was watching Hiya and Cynth ransacking Maeb's cabin in the Otherworld. Using their faerie dust, they knocked over lamps, upturned the sofa, and busted doors off their hinges. Chaos grabbed their wrists, shaking her head.

As much as destroying Maeb's home might make them feel self-satisfied, it wouldn't help them find Alden. Getting the message, the sprites nodded and continued the search with less destruction. Room after room turned out to be empty until the whole first floor was searched.

Hiya and Cynth raced ahead upstairs, but they came down before Chaos was finished checking the backyard. Shaking their heads "no," their tiny eyes brimmed with tears. Chaos, however, looked angry.

She swirled her hands, creating a cloud of faerie dust around her, but, before she could do anything, the doorknob began to turn. Chaos spun to aim her magic at the entrance. Hiya and Cynth hugged each other. They looked at the door with large, frightened eyes.

"Wait!" Cameron stood in the doorway with his hands up. A confused looking sidhe stood behind him (or an angry one). It was difficult to tell with Varick which of his emotions were not pent up rage. He placed a hand on the hilt of his sword.

Looking around, he said, "What are you little ones doing here?"

"Have you found Alden?" Cameron asked.

Chaos nodded. She began to gesture frantically.

Varick shook his head. "Slow yourself. I cannot understand your confounded hand-waving."

Cameron said, "Sorry, Chaos, I'm not as versed in your signs as Carissa. What are you trying to say?"

Chaos pointed behind them. A voice came from the opposite end of the living room. "Is this clear to you?" Maeb stood in the doorway with her grey magic encompassing her arms. She said, "I am really not in the mood to have visitors."

Chaos slapped her forehead. Hiya and Cynth took fighting stances that were more adorable than intimidating. They provided enough of a distraction for Varick to unsheathe his sword and lash out.

Maeb caught Varick's arm. The back of her hand landed in his face, smacking him to the ground. With a vicious smile, her magic shot out, but before Maeb's attack could find its target, Hiya and Cynth shot their faerie dust in her face. She coughed and waved what, to her, was just glittery air pollution. Varick swung again, but Chaos shook her head and tugged at his sleeve.

Hiya and Cynth were in full-on fighting mode now, attacking swiftly from every angle, which allowed Cameron to push Maeb out the door and shut it. Then he headed back indoors, following Chaos and the sprites upstairs.

"I will not run," Varick said, turning back.

"You want to die? How does that help Alden? Come on," Cameron said.

Between Cameron's hand on his arm and Chaos zapping him repeatedly toward the stairs, he sighed, sheathed his sword, and followed them upstairs. Once on the second floor, Chaos led them to the master bedroom and closed the double doors, tipping over a dresser to use as a barricade.

Varick scowled. "I will not hide away during a fight."

Chaos barely glanced at him, annoyed, then continued out to the deck. Once outside, there was nowhere else to go, unless one considered jumping onto the nearby redwood. It leaned close enough to the house for one to see the knots of wood that might serve as footfalls.

"Where are you leading us?" Cameron asked the sprite. She pointed upward.

"What? No. Alden cannot possibly be up there."

But the nature faeries raced ahead, leaving him no choice. He jumped onto the redwood and began to climb. Varick grunted and heaved himself onto the wood. He landed on the bark and rolled. Then dashed across the branch of the redwood tree and outpaced Cameron to the top.

Cameron sighed. "Of course you can do that." He looked up at their destination. Following Varick's path with his eyes, he spied the target of their climb. "A portal?" he whispered.

He let go of the tree and slid back onto the branch. Chaos look down, putting her hands on her hips. She may have scolded him, cut Cameron closed his eyes and reappeared right beside her. She blinked, then nodded as if approving.

Varick reached the final branch. He landed with a thump and walked the last stretch to them. Turning to Cameron, he asked, "Did you install a changeling portal above your home?"

Cameron said, "Not unless Tabitha snuck one in, which, come to think of it, she might have done."

"Where are we going?" Varick asked.

Chaos answered by grasping the button of his tunic sleeve and pulling him through it. Cameron followed, with Hiya and Cynth riding his jacket sleeves.

On the other side, they tumbled into a dark room. Varick stood, orienting himself and squinting in the low light.

"Little faerie?" Varick asked.

A grunt and thud proved Cameron had made it into the room.

Tonics and Turning Points

Faerie dust sparked once, then twice, then the soft glow of a torch on the wall flickered to life. Seeing Chaos light a torch gave the others the idea to do the same. Faerie fire lit the room, revealing their location.

Varick named it. "The Sidhe Council chambers in the great Redwood. But these cobwebs, this disrepair."

He reached out, pulling cobwebs away. Chaos lit more faerie lights as Varick walked across the room. He puzzled to himself as he went.

"Of course, no sidhe has died in Moss Hill as yet. So, the chambers would be unused in the World Beyond, wouldn't they?" He asked Chaos.

But Chaos's attention went to the middle of the room. As Cameron's eyes traced her gaze, he saw it, too. He rushed to the man lying in the center of the floor.

"Alden!" he called out.

Alden did not respond. He lay on his back, drained, cold to the touch, and unmoving. Varick unsheathed his blade. He held it under Alden's nose.

It was the afterlife, so there was no telling whether this would work. But it was the only way Varick knew to check if he was...if not alive, then a still-existing spirit. Chaos and the sprites peered intensely at the sword. Breath appeared on the blade.

Alden's soul, spirit, whatever he was, was still intact. Varick placed the sword back in its hilt and Cameron called out to him again. When Alden didn't respond, Varick tapped his cheek.

"Ankou, you must wake up."

"We'll have to carry him out," Cameron said.

Chaos's eyes welled, and she looked at him with a round-eyed spritely stare. Varick reached into his pocket and retrieved a vial. Chaos tilted her head curiously.

"What is that?" Cameron asked.

"Immortality elixir. I had hoped to give it to Jane eventually...I have to try. There is no other solution."

He searched Chaos's face as if he needed her approval. He might have valued the sprite's opinion at that moment as much as any sidhe elder. Varick had kept the elixir close to him all these months, had faced trouble for making it, and was ready now to use it for someone on whom it might not work. But it was Jane's brother, and Jane would be devastated if her brother were stuck in a helpless state in the World Beyond. Varick had no choice but to use the tonic to save him.

He lowered the vial and tilted it against Alden's lips. The green liquid flowed into his mouth and down his throat. He swallowed reflexively. Varick stood, and Chaos clutched his shoulder. Both waited, peering at Alden with bated breath.

Alden's eyes shot open. His form wavered between skeletal and human, each time his eyes changing from black as night to blue as day with flecks of gold. He jolted to a sitting position, sucking in air and clutching his chest.

"Wha-What did you do?" Alden asked when he had finally settled on his human form.

Varick reached a hand out to help Alden to his feet. Then he explained, "I'm not sure. I didn't know if it would work on an ankou."

He showed Alden the bottle with the handwritten label. Alden gripped the collar of Varick's tunic, "How could you? Do you realize what you've done?"

Cameron put a hand on both men's shoulders. "He was trying to help you."

Varick seized Alden's wrist and shoved it off. "I restored you from Maeb's magic. I've brought you back to life."

"Life? I can't be brought back to life. But now I can't enter the World Beyond. I'm not supposed to be ankou forever."

"So, you remain our ankou?" Varick asked.

"Worse than an ankou. You've turned me into a wraith—those who try to gain immortality but fail. I am undead."

"What does that mean?" Cameron asked.

Tonics and Turning Points

A feminine voice responded, "It means he is even more powerful than before."

Varick unsheathed his sword and spun around to face the speaker. Maeb struck out, holding his sword in a swirling, ashen cloud. But Hiya and Cynth came through the portal, distracting Maeb just long enough for Chaos to slice through her magic with her entire body.

"Pesky insects!" Maeb screeched as Hiya, and Cynth tugged at her hair.

Varick freed himself of Maeb's grasp as she snatched the sprites from the air. Maeb threw them and Alden dove to catch them both. Varick's blade sliced through the air and he lunged at Maeb, catching her in the shoulder.

She let out a banshee's cry, and her magic lashed out like a tornado, a swirl of grey threatening to engulf them in its vortex. Alden activated the portal, sending Hiya and Cynth through. Then, he shouted, "Hurry!"

Varick snatched Chaos from the air before the grey cloud could reach her and jumped, feet first, through the alder-stone portal. Alden shot one well-aimed blast of black magic toward Maeb and jumped through the portal himself. Cameron followed in quick succession before Maeb's attack on the portal could hit him.

Through the glass in Jane's home, Carissa, Holly, and Jane could not see whether Maeb's attack had done any harm to the portal. But Jane quickly rerouted the glass to show Cameron, Varick, and the sprites in the church reviving.

"Where is Alden?" Jane asked.

The question was asked and answered in short succession as Alden appeared beside them. Cameron, Varick, Chaos, Hiya, and Cynth all disappeared from the view in the glass. They reappeared, one by one as Varick brought them all to Jane's home. Cold as death, they warmed themselves by the fire.

"Quick. They need reviving and I have just the thing for it," Holly said, ushering Jane to the kitchen.

"What is it?" Jane asked.

Astoria Wright

"What everyone needs on a cold, winter night: tall, soul-warming mugs of hot chocolate."

Chapter 15

Committed to the Truth

Maren and Reg made it to Jane's just as it began to snow. Three shivering sprites warmed themselves over the roaring fire on the mantle, and Carissa helped Holly hand out mugs of hot chocolate. Jane provided thimbles for the nature faeries to use as their own hot chocolate cups. They drank eagerly and dunked their thimbles in Cameron's cup for seconds.

"How could you see us?" Cameron asked, filling Hiya's cup for him, as the sprite was prone to messes.

"And did you see whether our attack had any effect on Maeb?" Varick asked as he took his drink from Jane.

Carissa pointed above the mantle, "We used the mirror as a looking glass. We didn't see what happened to Maeb, but I doubt she will give up yet."

The front door slammed. Macara and Raven entered, taking off their coats and gloves. Dropping her umbrella into a basket by the door, Raven complained, "There's no vessel in Moss Hill that we could find."

"Cameron, Varick, it's good to see you are back. And Alden, my dear boy, are you all right?" Macara asked.

Alden exchanged a glance with Varick before answering, "I'm fine."

They each compared notes on their experiences, but the conversation fell short of Carissa's ears. All of her attention had gone to a picture on the mantle. She lifted the frame and studied it.

"Carissa?" Cameron asked.

The room fell silent as everyone noticed the look on Carissa's face. Her jaw was hanging open. She shouldn't speak so bluntly, perhaps, in front of Jane and Alden, but the Everlys had proof of Finlay's existence she could not ignore.

"It's him," Carissa pointed a finger in the face of the tallest man, the culprit. "He's the one that was in the picture Miss Morgan showed me."

Jane walked closer, looking at the picture. "These are business associates of my great-grandfather in London, not Mossies. You must not be remembering properly." Jane held her hand out to take the picture back, but Carissa didn't let go.

"Maybe it's just someone who looks similar?" Maren suggested.

Cameron studied the photo over Carissa's shoulder. He scrolled through his phone, then brought up a picture, saying, "No, she's right. These were the pictures from the day the City Hall was officially opened. See the man on the far left? It's him."

Varick tugged the photo out of Carissa's hands. He handed it to Jane, and the two compared the images.

The comparison could only bring Jane to one conclusion. "Impossible," her whisper was barely audible.

Alden stood. Varick stepped aside, allowing Alden to see the picture and screen together over his sister's shoulder.

Carissa said, "I'm sorry, Jane. But this man, Finlay, I'm sure he had everyone fooled—including your family."

"No. You have it wrong," Jane said. She pointed to Finlay. "That man wasn't just a friend of our family, he and my grandfather were business partners. He had a grandson my father's age who died a few years ago. Since his own son was estranged and his grandson died, my grandfather inherited our business from him. So, you see, he had no heirs to carry on his family name."

"Was his family name Finlay?" Reg asked.

Jane looked at Alden. "What was he named?" Jane fiddled with a necklace, one with a tree insignia carved into a silver circle. Carissa had seen it once before, but couldn't recall where.

Alden said, "We know it. I know we know it. I can't remember."

"Perhaps because he enchanted you not to recall it," Macara said.

Jane retorted, "Or we just forgot. We know for sure that he never set foot in Moss Hill. My father had never even heard of Moss Hill until he met my mother in college. He's not a Mossie, and we're not associated with any Finlay's—you have it wrong." It may have been a trick of the light, but the silver pendant on Jane's neck appeared to glow.

Jane set the photo of her great-grandparents' business associates snugly into its spot on the mantle. The pendant about her neck was normal as ever. She was being suspicious of everything.

Carissa's voice, when it returned to her, was gentle. "I don't doubt you, Jane, but that *is* Paden Finlay. There's no way around that."

"We'll have to ask your father a few questions. Perhaps he inherited more than just a business," Raven said.

Jane's eyes teared as she looked questioningly at her. "Are you accusing my father of something?"

Carissa tried to talk Raven's accusation down, "The prediction was that Finlay's great-grandson would bring Maeb back to life—not an Everly."

Raven said, "If Finlay treated Mr. Everly as his own child, the prediction could transfer to him."

Tears streamed down Jane's face. Varick's arms wrapped around her, but she pushed him back. Defiant, she slapped the phone into Cameron's chest and said to Raven, "His great-grandson would be Alden, and my brother would never betray Moss Hill like that."

Alden looked at Carissa with sad, searching eyes. "I never meant to hurt you. But I understand if you don't trust me now."

Cameron's hand gripped Carissa's shoulder. "What do you mean?" He looked between them.

Carissa's mouth dipped into a frown. She hadn't told him about Alden's momentary betrayal. She wanted to say that, of course, she still trusted him but saying anything would only reveal what had happened in the Borderlands. She would never doubt his loyalty to Moss Hill. She saw how he had suffered at Maeb's hands. But she wasn't sure of anything right now. "Of your own free will, I don't think you'd ever harm Moss Hill. But your father was on Vale Mountain today. He was conspiring with Maeb."

"That's quite the coincidence." Raven set her cup on the coffee table and walked toward Carissa.

Macara looked at her, expectantly. "It's also quite the accusation."

"I saw him, too," Cameron said.

"And so did Tabitha." Carissa stood firm. She held her head high and touched Cameron's hand gratefully.

"Well, it seems I'm accused in my own home," Mr. Everly said. Everyone turned to look through the foyer, where he, Mrs. Everly, and Fudge were entering the house.

Mr. Everly removed his hat and scarf, handing them to Fudge, who already held his coat. Mrs. Everly removed her fur coat as well, and Fudge disappeared down the hall with them.

Entering the living room, Mr. Everly said, "If I must explain myself, I was on Vale Mountain meeting with Mrs. O'Brien."

"Yes, we know. But you were also at Tabitha's at the same time as Maeb," Carissa said.

Tonics and Turning Points

Mr. Everly looked genuinely horrified. "I did not see Maeb there."

"Why meet on Vale Mountain today? That's a bit suspicious, you have to admit," Reg said.

Mr. Everly walked up to the fireplace. Cameron and Carissa had to move aside to let him through. He adjusted the picture of his grandfather and then met Reg's eyes as if challenging him. His wife sat in the sofa chair by the fireplace, expressionless. Her eyes did not leave her husband.

The sprites on the ottoman stared with open mouths. Hiya might have spilled his hot chocolate, except that Holly tipped it back with a finger.

Mr. Everly said, "I wanted another look at it to see why Mrs. O'Brien is claiming the renovations made it more suitable for some secret enterprise rather than the tourist site I had worked out with her and the town."

"And do you have a connection to the Finlays?"

Carissa would not back down. Even when Mr. Everly's hardened stare landed on her, she kept her shoulders straight and her head high. He didn't look angry, but stern and disapproving were his usual expressions, and he didn't stray from them now.

"What kind of accusation is that?"

"She believes an old prophecy that a Finlay would reawaken Maeb applied to us," Alden said.

From his tone, it was hard to distinguish whether Alden was denying the idea or asking his father for an explanation. Mr. Everly answered by scoffing at the suggestion.

"So, I've been lying to this town since I came here, is that it? Am I forever branded as 'not a Mossie?' What haven't I done for this town? What standard would finally make me one of you?"

"Father, they're hurt and confused. I'm sure they wouldn't accuse you if not for that," Jane said.

"Perhaps if you talked to the Sidhe Council," Varick suggested.

Raven said, "Blast the politeness. The Sidhe Council should put you under lock and key while the guards do a thorough search of your possessions. And get a lawyer or whatever humans do." Macara swatted her shoulder. She was standing three feet away, so her tap was more of a gust of wind strong enough to give Raven a nudge.

"You can't arrest him with just a photograph of a friendship for proof. You wouldn't do that, would you?" Jane looked at Varick, then everyone else in the room one by one. She took a literal stand, holding her hands to her sides in such a way, Carissa knew she could summon her druid powers in a second.

The last thing Carissa wanted was a fight with a druid like Jane. She was formidable in her own right. Still, knowing now that Mr. Everly might also be, at the very least, an unwitting assistant to Maeb, made the situation all the more dangerous. Carissa put a hand on Cameron's arm, pleading for him to back down. It didn't matter if Mr. Everly was a pawn of Finlay's or not. At the moment, all that mattered was that Jane and Alden would defend him and Carissa did not want either of them hurt in a confrontation.

Carissa chose her words carefully. "We don't see you as an outsider, Mr. Everly. We were hoping for your help. You know London, you know Moss Hill, and you're well-traveled. Perhaps you have some insight into who might be helping Maeb?"

Mr. Everly adjusted his tie. He cleared his throat. "A reasonable request. Yes, I might be able to deduce it. Let's see, Belkin, for one, we know to be a changeling, perhaps he's not the original Belkin, but someone who returned from his last hunting trip in his guise? O'Brien, too, left Moss Hill for quite some time, and Mrs. O'Brien did act rather strange today."

"How so?" Cameron asked.

"She cut the meeting short, yelled at me, actually, for wasting her time. Then she hurried off. By the time I left Fairfield Castle, there was no trace of her car. And you know she doesn't drive that well, so her speeding away I can't say is a good sign."

Maren shrugged. "I saw Mrs. O'Brien at Gooseberry not a half-hour ago. She seemed fine to me."

Mr. Everly took the poker out of its holder. Resting an arm atop the mantle, he leaned casually over the fireplace and poked at the burning wood. "I must admit, it's not Mrs. O'Brien or Mr. Belkin who worry me." He replaced the poker and looked at Macara and Raven. "I overheard a rumor today, and I must say that it's more concerning to me that a Tuatha de Danann might have helped Maeb stay half-alive all these years."

"Where did you hear that?"

"I heard there were two Tuatha de Danann quibbling about all through town."

Raven rolled her eyes. "Good gracious!"

Macara flashed her a glance. *Of course they heard you and your loud mouth.*

Mr. Everly walked to his son, putting an arm around him. He held his other hand out to call his daughter over. She walked to him. Even Mrs. Everly went to his side, embracing him and Jane with a motherly affection that seemed foreign to her.

"You may no longer trust me, but I trusted you, all of you. I let you into my home only to discover that one of you may have offered Maeb a chance to return to life? Did you also conspire with the sidhe to target my daughter last year? Or perhaps you poisoned my son? It seems clear to me now that someone is targeting my family." Mr. Everly looked Cameron directly in the eye. "I don't have to tell you how concerning that is to me, do I? As a husband and a father, I demand that you treat that as your top priority. I'm sorry, Macara, Raven. I want you out of this house until I determine who I can trust."

Raven's eye twitched, and she looked like she might launch into a tirade that might end in the house exploding or at least cause damage to some priceless heirlooms. But Macara clutched her forearm and pulled her back. Raven caught the warning in Macara's eyes, and both sisters left without a word. Holly followed behind in a hurry. Jane, though teary-eyed, did not protest.

"We'll leave, too. Sorry to have bothered you," Cameron said, taking Carissa's hand. The nature fairies left their perch, as well. Reg and Maren followed their lead. Cameron looked at Alden. "If you need us, you know where we'll be."

Alden nodded. The Everlys watched Fudge lead them to the door. Fudge's expression was even more sour than usual, but his heavy brow showed that the emotion was not anger. Even he was sad to kick them out.

It felt like something was wrong with the whole world. Not just because the sky was grey and rain or sleet or snow threatened to hit at any moment, but the entire situation felt...wrong. Outside, Macara, Raven, and Holly waited on the wet pavement. They walked to the two cars, all of them together.

"Do you believe him?" Carissa asked.

"Not for one moment," Raven said.

"They're definitely hiding something," Reg added.

"Not Jane and Alden, but Mr. Everly for sure," Maren agreed.

"He was hiding something." Cameron unlocked the doors and opening the driver's side.

Carissa opened her side for Holly. Reg and Maren took their car.

"Where are we going?" They asked.

"My home," Macara said. The two nature faeries settled on her shoulders. Chaos settled on Raven's. Macara disappeared first.

Before she left, Raven said, "We can't know anything for sure unless we talk to someone on the other side."

"Who?" Reg asked.

"I think it's time we have a chat with our dearly departed sister," Raven said as she faded from view.

Chapter 16

Dream of a Funeral

Macara opened the curtains on the window in her cottage home. Raven prepared the fae fire while Holly chopped up the mistletoe for arranging in the window. Macara placed her palms on the glass, closed her eyes, and concentrated on the spell to open a vision to the Otherworld.

Raven, behind her, quibbled with Chaos. "Oh, all right. Just be careful."

The nature faerie flew from her perch on Raven's shoulder into the fireplace.

"Chaos!" Carissa would have rushed forward had Cameron's hand not caught her around the waist.

Raven put a palm up. "It's fae fire. She's fine."

It wasn't green like a fae fire. Carissa had always thought the reddish-orange flame in Macara's home was a regular fire. She should have known that in a Tuatha de Danann's home nothing was as it seemed. When Chaos emerged from the flame, she was glowing like an ember.

Hiya's and Cynth's jaws fell and their eyes bugged out of their heads. Minds blown, the nature faeries watched Chaos glide to the window pane. Macara stepped away, allowing

Chaos to touch the glass. She pressed her hands to the center of a pane.

The pulsating glow rippled through Chaos's body and into the glass. It traveled in waves until the fading light of day gave way to the view of Jane's room.

"The Everly's mansion?" Holly asked.

"Why would she be there?" Cameron whispered.

"Do you really think she could be in league with Maeb?" Maren asked.

"You heard Mr. Everly cast suspicion on his son's death," Reg said.

"I thought that was strange for other reasons," Carissa said.

"What reasons?" Cameron asked.

She explained, "If Mr. Everly suspected his son's death was unnatural, why is he only bringing it up now? And if he thought Miss Morgan was involved, why let her stay in his home?"

Holly said, "Doesn't that mean he and Miss Morgan were on the same side? Whichever side that was."

Macara said, "No need to speculate until after we speak to our sister."

Reg said, "She isn't there, though. And why is it showing us the living world?"

"Do you not see the hue? We are not seeing the World Beyond. That eerie blend of light doesn't exist here." Holly shivered.

Raven stepped closer to the glass and tapped it with her index finger. Chaos flew to her shoulder. Her eyebrows knit together and she looked at Raven. Too busy with the glass, Raven ignored her concerned expression.

Macara said, "Don't worry, Chaos. You did nothing wrong. She must be there somewhere."

"Then show us." Raven flicked her palms toward the mirror.

The image zoomed to the other side of Jane's bedroom. There was Miss Morgan, standing over Jane's form as she sat at the windowsill in her night gown and silk robe. She was leaning against the wall in her bay window, reading some old volume.

Miss Morgan's hands traveled in the air over Jane's body. The tree insignia necklace glowed. This time Carissa knew it wasn't her imagination and she recalled where she'd seen the pendant before. Miss Morgan had once tried to barter it at the apothecary shop. From head to toe, grey clouds swirled over and through the druidess's form as she sat unaware of what was happening in the World Beyond.

"Maeb's magic!" Carissa called out.

"Caught red-handed!" Holly's shout caught Miss Morgan's attention. She stopped. The grey clouds disappeared. Miss Morgan walked to the mirror and rolled her eyes.

"Why are you spying on me?"

"Apparently because you warrant our spying. What are you doing?" Raven crossed her arms and Chaos, on her shoulder, made the same gesture.

"You said that the dead could not see the living," Carissa said.

"Special circumstances require special magic," Miss Morgan said.

"Like Maeb's magic? You traitor." Holly pointed a finger.

Macara pushed Holly's hand down and put a hand on Raven's free shoulder. "Sister, can you explain the grey magic?

"And don't you say it's yours," Raven said.

"It's not. That magic belongs to Maeb," she said matter-of-factly.

"She admits it." Holly wagged her finger this time.

Miss Morgan said, "If you shut up a second, I'll tell you that I saw your search for a vessel tying Maeb's soul to this world."

"Spying," Raven said under her breath. Or perhaps she had whispered it to Macara.

107

Undisturbed by the notion, Macara said, "Then you saw we could not find it."

"No, but you were right about the living link. It wasn't my birds, and thank you very much for your suspicions. I'm so glad you cared enough to remember that I was killed by the unseelie. And I don't recall you being at my funeral, Raven?"

Raven glanced at the floor, muttering, "Couldn't make it." She looked up, finding her argument, "Some of us take a more active role in saving the world than acting as nanny to a druid family."

"And have the Tuatha de Danann taken away your powers for that yet?" Miss Morgan zinged back.

Macara, the voice of reason, said, "What do you mean we were right about the living link? If it wasn't your birds, then what?"

"Not what. Who?" Miss Morgan pointed at Jane.

There was no more magic around her and she looked like herself. Carissa couldn't picture sweet Jane as anything but innocent. "What if it's not her? What if it's the necklace she's wearing?"

"That's a MacAirt heirloom. Bad luck, in my opinion, but nothing more than that. We should be more concerned that Maeb's soul might be in her."

"You mean Maeb is controlling her with her magic?" Maren asked.

"Who is that?" Miss Morgan asked.

Raven and Macara turned so that the humans behind them were all visible from the window. Maren raised a hand and gave a sheepish grin that shaped itself more like a grimace.

"The pink-eared one. As usual, you misunderstand me. You never could get my orders right."

"You never ordered anything that made sense." Maren's eyes widened as she realized she'd just talked back to a Tuatha de Danann in front of her two sisters. With them looking at her sharply, she gulped. She added with her hands up, "Sorry. No offense meant."

Tonics and Turning Points

"Hmph. Do I see Cari? I thought the vessel might be you for a second. Glad I was wrong. But if it was, I suppose she would have had possession of you already."

"Possession? Does that mean Jane is really Maeb?" Cameron asked.

Carissa loved the way Cameron's arms wrapped around her every time he thought she was in danger. He gripped her tightly now. But the danger wasn't aimed at her.

"She isn't possessed yet. The link is there in the background. She might be using Jane as her vessel, and, if so, she could use that to her advantage."

Though his opinion wasn't required, Reg said, "I agree. It would strengthen the bond, which would only give Maeb an in to take over Jane's body."

"No." Macara's stern voice cut through the air. "Jane is not weak. She would not allow Maeb to take over her body."

Miss Morgan said, "Even strong people can be made weak."

"She may not be able to fight Maeb forever," Raven said.

"We could lock her magic. Cari could be the protector of Moss Hill, at least until we find a way to keep Jane safe from Maeb." Holly suggested.

"Locking Jane's magic would make her defenseless against the part of Maeb's soul that's already inside her," Macara said.

"You're both insufferable! Will you hush? I'm not suggesting Jane's magic be sealed, I'm suggesting removing Maeb's magic from her. One of you needs to steal it," Miss Morgan said.

Raven smiled. "Brilliant."

"Also against the rules, but we seem to be breaking those today," Macara said.

"Might makes right. The ends justify the means, and so on. Whichever idiom gets you agree to." Raven waved her hand with her wrist in a "so on and so forth" manner.

"Rules have reasons. And where we have reason to break them, we must," Miss Morgan said. "The only way to free Jane and ensure Maeb is stuck in the World Beyond forever is for Jane to take the magic Maeb has embedded in her *out of her*, or sever it from Maeb completely."

"But how did Maeb tie her magic to Jane in the first place? Was it the Tuatha de Danann accomplice who did that?" Cameron asked.

The three sisters' expressions turned grim. A long while passed in which they could only hear the beating of rain outside and the whistling of the wind. Miss Morgan ended the silence with a grunt.

"I know what you're thinking and it's not him."

Raven threw her hands down. "It has to be. There's no other possibility."

"He has connected himself to the Everly family," Holly said.

"And he appointed Alden as ankou of Moss Hill. For two years, I might add, one longer than an ankou is supposed to serve," Raven added.

"We can't know for sure it's him." Macara started at the window pane, as if considering.

Maren said, "Who are you talking about."

"MacLir," Carissa said. She looked at Raven, Macara, and Miss Morgan for confirmation. They each nodded. Carissa turned to Maren, Reg, and Cameron, explaining, "He controls the gates between our worlds, the Borderlands, and the World Beyond. If Maeb really wanted to come back to the land of the living, he'd be the Tuatha de Danann to ask."

Miss Morgan said, "I'm telling you it isn't him. He would not betray us."

"And you did not, either? Then, who?" Raven asked.

"Maybe no one. Did you think of that? It doesn't matter now, anyway. Jane is waking. She might sense me and I don't want to be here when she does."

Tonics and Turning Points

Miss Morgan ended the connection by reaching her hand on the mirror. From their perspective, her hand grew to giant size over the window frame. Then, it vanished.

The scene faded in the window, leaving a dark image behind it.

"Who is that?" Reg asked.

"Is someone with her?" Maren asked.

"It's a man of some kind," Cameron observed.

But Carissa picked up the silhouette's true location, "That's not in the Borderlands. That's here." A flash of lightning illuminated the figure.

It was a Tuatha de Danann: Manann MacLir.

Chapter 17

Heart of the Matter

The knocks on the door made Maren jump. Side by side on the couch, Reg put a calming hand on Maren's lap. Raven drew her magic to her fingertips, the purple haze forming before Holly could walk to the door.

"Stop that." Macara smacked Raven's hand.

Holly would have answered but her phone dinged, causing her to first jump, then scratch her head, looking at the screen confused.

Macara answered the door.

MacLir took off his hat, like a gentleman, and said, "May I come in?"

Stepping back, Macara allowed him to enter and took his hat and coat to set on the hangers.

"What are you doing here?" Raven refused to sit.

Though Holly had joined Reg and Maren on the couch, Cameron and Carissa took the window seat, and Macara and MacLir sat on the sofa chairs by the fire.

"In Moss Hill or in this home?" MacLir asked.

"Both," Raven said with a hint of violence in her eyes. Macara didn't stop her as she'd done with Miss Morgan. Was that because she suspected him more?

MacLir unbuttoned his blazer, relaxing into the back of the seat. He nodded at Reg. "This one called me."

Cameron looked at Reg, saying, "How could you?"

Reg stumbled on his words, "I didn't know…I mean I, how was I to suspect that he…that he…."

"What's wrong with him working with me?" MacLir asked.

Maren scooched away from Reg. "You're still working for him? Was being the mayor an excuse to spy for him?"

"I worked with him to help Moss Hill! I swear I didn't know he was working for Maeb!" Reg pleaded, grasping Maren's hands.

Holly held up her cell phone. Or did you? That would explain these words that appeared here by magic: *Modern descendent is Roger Finlay, currently deceased.* That means you, sir are an ankou!" She pointed at Reg.

Reg looked flabbergasted, "My name is Reg Smith and I am certainly not dead!"

"Why would my celly-phone say your name is Roger Finlay then?" Holly asked.

Reg shot back, "That's not my name! And if you want to shoot accusations around: Why did you say you were giving Carissa a tonic and then one mysteriously appeared in her dressing room that ended up almost killing her!"

Carissa reached for the phone, "May I see that, please?"

Holly got up, stomped over the to the kitchen, took out her purse, and flashed a tonic in front of them all. "*This* is my calming tonic. I would never poison Cari. You, however—"

Carissa stepped between Holly's accusing finger and Reg's bewildered expression. "I asked Tilly to text us about Finlay's descendant's name. It may be similar to Reg's, but it is not the same. The articles she linked to had pictures of the man. He looked nothing like Reg."

Holly, Cameron, and Maren all looked. Reg took the phone after them. "He looks a little like Alden, if I'm honest."

Holly rolled her eyes. "Now you're just making things up."

MacLir said, "Enough. Mr. Everly tells me that there is a terrible lack of trust amongst you and I'm sorry to see he was right. Is that why you stormed out of Mr. Everly's home?" MacLir acted like this was the first he'd heard of the accusation.

"We were kicked out," Raven said.

MacLir's eyebrows darted together, and his hand found a way to his chin. "With the way you're accusing each other and him, I'm not surprised."

"Let us dismiss another accusation then: Do you deny tying Maeb's soul to the living world?" Macara got to the heart of the matter.

MacLir's hand fell away, and he held Macara's gaze for a long time. Carissa could see it in his eyes. The guilt, no, the regret.

"You don't deny it, do you? You can't," Carissa said.

He glanced at her briefly, then away, into the fire. "I felt responsible for Maeb's destruction. I don't just mean her death, her downward spiral into misguided ambition. She lost her father when she was young. She was given a position she wasn't ready to handle, overseeing a province back in the days when the Tuatha de Danann ruled Ireland. She had ambition as if she had something to prove. And I thwarted every attempt she made to dominate the humans. I never took the time to explain, to help her understand. But one of her sons, I could reach him."

"The wayward son." Raven nodded. She looked at Carissa, saying, "Your great-grandfather. Maeb made me promise to protect him. Though, I didn't know she meant for me to protect him from you."

MacLir laughed. "You'd have made a formidable foe, had we not, ultimately, been on the same side. Seeing your attempts to persuade Maeb to see reason made me realize that

I hadn't made any such attempt. On her deathbed, when she asked for a chance to be redeemed, I felt I had to give it to her."

"But she died a century before Jane was born," Cameron said. He volunteered more information than was asked. "A jealous woman whose husband Maeb had had an affair with shot her."

MacLir wasn't interested in the recounting of her death. "What has Jane to do with it?"

"Maeb is tied to the living world through Jane," Macara said.

MacLir stood, pacing. "No, I did not link her to a living soul."

"To what, then?" Raven asked.

MacLir sat on the edge of his chair, speaking with his hands, with his whole body animated. "I split Maeb's essence into three to make it difficult for her to return to the living world with my help. I tied her mind to a tree in Tara, her magic to a talisman, and her soul to the *Scuabtuinne's* Immortal Flame. There is no way for her to be here."

"Yet, she is here in Moss Hill," Raven said.

"And she has her magic," Cameron added.

"I think this talisman released it by stealing mine." Carissa held up the Talisman of Tethra, which she still could not remove.

MacLir reach out and touched it. "This is what I feared. The Immortal Flame changed color on its return from Moss Hill, and here you have the talisman containing her magic. So, she has the two. Only essence remains in Tara."

"I think that part is in Jane now. If it wasn't you who linked her with Maeb, then how is she connected?" Reg asked.

MacLir released the talisman and Carissa with it. "Her will is no longer locked in the talisman. I hate to distrust my own ankou, but linking a spirit to a person would require the person to be in the World Beyond. Which is why, forgive me, but I would have thought Maeb would tie herself to Carissa and not Jane."

"Carissa is free of Maeb's powers, Cameron made certain of that," Macara said.

Carissa said, "What if she's not tied to Jane, though? You said it was a tree Maeb is tied to in Tara. Jane has a pendant with the insignia of a tree. What if the pendant is somehow linked with the tree in Tara?"

MacLir waved the question away. "The MacAirt pendant was created by her druid ancestors as an heirloom reminding them of a prophetic dream about Cormac MacAirt's birth. It is the same type of tree, but that is as far as the comparison goes."

Glances passed between all of them. If they were all thinking the same way as Carissa, they each wondered whether they could trust him.

"With respect, I don't understand why you would give Maeb a chance at all. Hadn't she proven in life that she was evil?"

Raven said, "'Evil' *is a made-up word that allows you to think of yourself as 'good.'* It makes the world simple and, therefore, safe. But the world is not simple. And by no means should you ever be fooled into thinking it is safe."

"It's safer with Maeb on the other side of it," Holly said.

"She wasn't always so dangerous," Raven said.

"You would know that better than anyone." MacLir's tone was accusatory.

Carissa knew she ought to leave it alone, but she wanted to hear the story, if for nothing else, then at least to put the matter to rest. "Maeb said that you were friends once."

Raven straightened her shoulders haughtily. "Yes. We were. We were both strong enough to understand that sometimes battles had to be fought with conviction or not at all. But I changed. I learned and came to understand humans. I even like some of you, sometimes. She didn't. I'm sorry there's no more of a story to fuel your suspicions, but that sometimes the facts are ordinary and dull."

Cameron said, "Let's suppose we believe you both. If it wasn't either of you, then we only have the prophecy of Paden Finlay that his great-grandson would bring Maeb back."

"But the last Finlay descendent is dead and the closest thing to him would be Alden. I don't believe he could do something like that," Maren said.

Carissa said, "Not of his own free will. I fear Maeb might still have a hold over him and if she's got a hold of Jane's pendant, she might also be under Maeb's control. I'm not accusing them, but I think we need to save them."

Raven spoke over her own shoulder, "Chaos, fetch Alden. We must get to the bottom of this tonight."

* * *

ALDEN ARRIVED SURROUNDED by a wave of fog. His magic dissipated around him in black wisps, revealing that Jane and Varick were with him. But, Alden, whose ankou form generally had a frightening effect, was changed. Instead of the skeletal form Carissa was used to seeing, Alden's skin remained human. But his eyes were black. They cleared to blue in seconds. Still, the effect struck them all as terrifying.

"Your magic…it's different," Carissa said.

Alden shared a glance with Varick, and it hit her how much the elixir had changed him. To the others, she knew this would look bad. She wanted to explain that it was not Maeb's magic that had changed Alden. But Varick spoke first.

"Why has your little faerie brought us here?"

"She summoned Alden and Jane, not you," Raven said.

"I am protecting the Everly family tonight as my sworn duty as a sidhe guard."

Jane replied, "I prefer him to be here and MacLir, too."

"You can trust them, Jane," MacLir said gently.

"But can we trust you?" Raven asked.

"Raven," Macara reprimanded.

Holly stifled a sob. Macara stood and gestured affectionately for Jane to take her chair. She stood by Jane's side as they all explained that Maeb had bound herself to her. Jane's eyes teared as the revelation sunk it.

Jane opened the robe of her dressing gown enough to show that she'd removed the pendant, "I don't wear it all the time. I don't think it's the pendant, I think it's me. I never felt fully in control of my powers."

"You weren't trained until after my death," Alden said.

Jane shook her head. "No, Alden. I can feel it. I'm sorry, Varick, but that is why I never wanted to be immortal. There are times I just don't feel myself. I never could explain it until now."

Raven said, "It may be why that sidhe tried to poison you and why Warren targeted you. You're a danger to the seelie and a savior to the unseelie as long as you are Maeb's living connection to the world."

Varick growled, "Stop."

Macara said, "For goodness sakes, Raven, can't you see she's crying?"

Through tears, Jane said, "No, she's right. As long as I'm alive, Maeb will have a connection to this world."

"Not as long as you're alive, my dear. Did I say, 'As long as you're alive?' No—as long as you are connected to Maeb, that is the key."

"How do we break the connection?" Varick asked.

"Kill her," Raven said.

Jane paled, and Carissa gasped.

"Oh, for the love of...." Holly rubbed her forehead.

Even Macara sounded like she might lose her temper. "Must you say things in the most dramatic fashion? We're not going to kill Jane. We're going to kill Maeb."

"That's what I said." Raven gave a wide-eyed expression.

Alden asked, "How do we kill Maeb?"

Carissa felt nauseous at the idea of killing anyone. But Maeb was already dead, wasn't she? So, it wasn't so much that killing her as it was undoing her undead status.

Jane said, almost breathlessly, "Killing me would work."

Carissa's voice was flat and firm, "No one is killing anyone. But you are going to have to break a fae law by stealing her magic."

Varick agreed, with some persuasion, to put aside his strict adherence to the law. For the sake of love, both for Jane and the island, he could step out of the role of sidhe guard—just this once. Alden accepted the duty of taking Maeb to the World Beyond for good once her powers were stripped. Jane was the less willing one.

"Are you certain I'm powerful enough to steal Maeb's magic?" Jane asked.

"In this world, you are the more powerful one, because it is your body and your life."

"But there are many powerful people in Moss Hill. I still don't understand why she'd choose me."

"Because we're druids on both sides. Carissa was right about the picture. We are connected to the Finlays."

"What are you saying? Spit it out," Raven said.

"I'm sorry, Jane. Edris Everly is not our father. Mother erased my memory of our real father, Roger Finlay. Maybe she thought it was too painful. All I needed was the reminder tonight and the memories came flooding back. I was five and you were not yet born when he died. Mr. Everly stepped in to take our place. I learned to speak and think and act and dress like Edris Everly, but deep down I always knew he wasn't my father.

"Our real father wanted out of Grandpa Finlay's control. All of it, even marrying our mother was a role picked out for him. But it was a role our stepfather was more than happy to fill," Alden said.

"Because he loved our mother? You can't mean anything else." Jane asked it with hope, rather than saying it with conviction. But there was a sad tone to it like she knew the answer.

"Because he loved money or power or both. I could see through him, Jane. And he knew it all this time that I was so close to remembering. That's why he wanted me out of the way. Now it all makes sense." A cloud of black surrounded him.

"Alden?" Varick asked.

"Do not do anything foolish." MacLir stood.

Alden disappeared before he could make it one step past the chair.

"Where did he go?" Jane asked.

"To do something that he can't take back." MacLir used his magic to make an exit, as well.

"Hurry," Raven said, reaching her hand out to Holly and Jane. Macara did the same for Carissa and Cameron while the sprites held on tight where they were.

"What about us? Where are you going?" Reg called out.

Raven, Jane, and Holly disappeared.

As Marcara readied her magic to follow them, Carissa said, "Back to the Everly mansion. Alden is going to confront his killer."

Chapter 18

Domestic Hostility

Mr. Everly narrowly dodged a blast of magic from his son. He was not so lucky on the second blow. In the dim light of his study, Everly gasped for air as his stepson's hand squeezed his throat. In only his nightclothes and robe, Everly seemed defenseless against him. MacLir, who had arrived first, pulled Alden off him, physically holding him back by the chest.

Alden shouted with such rage he spit as he talked. The black in his eyes returned and his voice changed to a wraithlike depth, "Don't pretend. You're a druid, too. I saw you doing magic the night you visited me in college. Before you poisoned me, you were using a window to conspire with my grandfather to kill me."

Mr. Everly coughed and breathed in dry heaves. Jane could only cry and cling to Varick. Carissa and Cameron watched, uncertain what to do.

Still grasping Alden's arm, MacLir said, "You cannot just attack him like this. Let us take him to the Sidhe Council."

"You and my grandfather, you killed my father to get him out of the way because he didn't agree with what you were all doing!"

Mrs. Everly appeared in the doorway and gasped. She found her way to her husband's side and bent, clutching his shoulders. Alden struggled against MacLir's grip.

"Get away from him, mother. He's dangerous."

Mrs. Everly looked to Macara and Raven, "What's happening to my son? What has come over him?"

"He's a druid, mother. He killed our father. He killed me. He'll kill Jane, too."

Poor Mrs. Everly glanced at each of their faces questioningly, but kept her arms around her husband. He finally caught his breath, managing to get out a handful of words. They were meaningless, until Carissa realized it was a spell—a healing spell.

Jane clutched Varick's tunic. Wide-eyed, she shook her head in disbelief. Macara and Raven exchanged glances and Carissa wished she had her magic. Cameron stepped in front of her, protecting her from this stranger they thought they knew.

Watching Mr. Everly use magic was the most frightening sight Carissa had ever witnessed. This man whom everyone knew to be human was, in fact, a druid. And now that he was healed, he wore a terrible vengeance on his face.

Calm as the eye of a storm, Mr. Everly met his son's glare. Retying his robe, Mr. Everly stood and shared a glance with his wife. She nodded in some unspoken understanding.

Mrs. Everly said, "Alden, you're upset. Let's all sit down together and we can discuss this rationally."

Alden's eyes returned to a crystal blue. "You knew?"

"An explanation seems due," Macara said.

"There is nothing to explain," Mr. Everly said.

"You deny Alden's accusation?" Carissa asked.

The Everlys said nothing.

"Let me go," Alden demanded. Since he had taken a human form, he seemed himself.

MacLir released his grip on his shoulders.

Tonics and Turning Points

Alden walked to his sister. "You aren't getting to Jane. She isn't staying here anymore. Varick, you can send some sidhe to collect her things tomorrow."

Varick nodded. With Varick pulling at one hand and her other arm in Alden's grasp, Jane looked at her mother, upset.

Mrs. Everly shook her head. "Jane," she said affectionately, "You don't have to go."

Jane stood firm. "Why am I tied to Maeb?" she asked.

"Don't, Jane," said Alden.

"Leave the matter to the Tuatha de Danann," Varick said.

"I want to know. I want an answer." She wouldn't release her parents from her gaze.

Carissa could understand why they wanted Jane out of there. But she was also glad to see Jane standing up for herself. She'd shown herself to be a powerful druid. But her strength of will had always hidden behind a meek nature.

Raven pushed herself between Jane and the Everlys. "You'll explain to us or to the Sidhe Council. Either way, your daughter is leaving now."

Mr. Everly batted Alden and Varick away from Jane with a wave of his hand. His magic was an invisible force, which dragged Jane from his office to the adjoining bedroom. The double doors slammed, locking her inside.

Mrs. Everly, who had not used the druidic art since her son's birth, instinctively created a barrier of air protecting her husband against MacLir's attack. It was no match for a Tuatha de Danann. She and Mr. Everly dodged in time for a beam of white light to blast a hole in the bookcase behind them. Carissa clutched the talisman around her neck as Cameron pushed her behind him and out of the fight.

Raven shook her head. "Fools. There are three Tuatha de Danann against you. No druid is strong enough to fight us."

"Two druids. Three, if you join us Alden," Mrs. Everly said.

"Mother, why are you helping him?" Alden pulled Varick to his feet.

Jane banged against the doors. Varick tried his magic against the lock, but it wouldn't budge. He turned and stared at Mr. Everly, baring his teeth as if he might bite his head off.

Mr. Everly said, "She was never for you, Varick. Jane has a greater life planned for her than any of us."

"Is it money or power that made you betray your own children?" Alden's veins throbbed. Wraith magic writhed beneath the surface, bulging through the muscles of his arms and neck, traveling to his face.

It made Carissa and Cameron step back. But Mrs. Everly walked forward. She reached for his cheek. He jerked back. Her teary eyes stopped his from turning color.

"Do you recall the story of our ancestor Cormac MacAirt?" she asked.

MacLir chided her, "Cormac was a good man who went on to become a great king. He wasn't a supporter of malcontents like Maeb."

Mrs. Everly's stared icily at MacLir. "He met Maeb because of you. You took him to the World Beyond, and he came back changed. He left part of his soul in that world—and he taught his family how to sacrifice a part of themselves to help save the rest of the world."

"Maeb was already connected to your family. She didn't just recruit the Finlays. She also had the MacAirts allied with her." Carissa realized.

"She connected herself to our ancestor, and her power helped him create a prosperous kingdom. It was then he realized that only when you have true power can you create true peace. The Tuatha de Danann were meant to rule over the druids and druids, in turn, should rule over the humans. Think how peaceful the world would be if you were in charge, MacLir. Raven, Macara, think of the good you could do if you persuaded the council to come out of hiding."

"Ridiculous. You've had this notion the whole time? You learned nothing from our sister?" Raven asked.

Tonics and Turning Points

Mrs. Everly smiled. "Your sister never stopped prattling on about how she disliked the humans. And strong as she was, she never sensed that Jane was connected to Maeb from birth, and I before her. The connection transfers to every daughter down the line of Cormac MacAirt's descendants. When I was pregnant with Jane, it passed from me to her. That's why Jane is so powerful.

"But it was only a small fragment of Maeb. It wasn't until recently, when the *Scuabtuinne* last touched our shores that my husband was able to get the remaining shard of Maeb's power. We have enough to restore her. All we need is to suppress Jane's powers for Maeb to gain control. Unless Cari, you volunteer yourself as her vessel."

Cameron broadened his chest. "Never."

"Then you leave us no choice." Mr. Everly opened the library doors. An invisible force snatched the talisman off Carissa's neck. Mrs. Everly's hand controlled its trajectory, winding it around Jane's neck.

"Two birds with one Talisman. Without the talisman's protection, you die

"Cari!" Cameron caught her as she fell. Her eyes fluttered as she felt her magic swell against that of the poison within her. It burned. She writhed in pain on the floor.

Macara stood over her, shouting directions. "Hold her hands. You'll have to share in her magic and in the poison."

Cameron pressed his hands in hers.

She felt the pain release in a flow away from her heart to his. "No," she managed, looking at Cameron. She didn't want him to take on her pain. What would it do to him? She tried to focus on his face, which contorted, but her eyes couldn't focus.

Behind him, Maeb's grey magic appeared in a streaming blast.

Carissa traced it from an object in Mr. Everly's hand to the center of Jane's chest. It was Jane's tree-shaped pendant. The very amulet Jane had worn to protect her was the artifact the Everlys had sealed with Maeb's magic. With the talisman around Jane's neck and the pendant aimed at her, Jane's magic would be drained and Maeb's essence would be free to flow into Jane's body.

Vaguely, MacLir and Raven's voices shot above her head.

"No, Alden!" MacLir shouted.

"Stupid! You save him, I've got her," Raven said.

Carissa turned her head, catching sight of Raven knocking Mrs. Everly unconscious. To her left, Alden was caught in Maeb's magic. He had gotten in the middle of the stream from Jane's pendant to the talisman. Varick struck the magic around Jane with his sword, to no avail.

Mr. MacLir wrenched Alden from the stream and attempted to heal him.

"Help her!" Varick screamed.

Carissa tried to stand. Though Cameron looked pale, he asked, "Are you all right?"

"Don't use your magic yet," Macara said.

"I have to," Carissa said, breathlessly.

Behind her, in the doorway, Fudge appeared.

"No, get back." Carissa managed to stand enough to shield him. But he held her arms and moved her to the side. Standing in front of her, Fudge looked across the room, taking in the action.

Raven's magic twisted with Maeb's, battling it off successfully. But Jane was still in the line of fire. Fudge rushed in between them, as Alden must have done before him.

"Why is everyone so foolish?" Raven shouted. She warned, "Stay out of this, Fudge."

"My name is Fíodóir Draíochta," Fudge said.

With the mention of his true name, his eyes glowed, and, with one look, Mr. Everly flew to the back of the room and out the sliding doors. They heard the glass shatter before seeing it fly out from the curtain. Mr. Everly disappeared, far into the garden, creating a groove in the snow. Carissa could no longer see him. She turned back to Fudge.

Tonics and Turning Points

The Rhys Dwfen magic was a sight. Fudge almost looked like a spirit in a cyclone of yellow light. Macara left Carissa to join her sister in circling around Fudge.

"Now you've done it," Raven said.

Macara stroked his shoulder, soothing him. "Calm yourself."

Fudge's eyes returned to their normal, dark tone. He walked to Jane's side, saying only, "I am calm."

Raven rushed outside.

"Jane? Jane." Alden held his sister. She didn't respond.

Macara touched her wrist. "The pulse is weak."

Fudge reached toward Jane's neck. With his hand lit, he pulled the talisman off it. His magic was strong enough to remove it easily.

Something felt wrong. Carissa's heart pounded in her chest. She and Cameron held onto each other, watching helplessly. With the talisman removed, Jane's magic should have been restored to heal her. That was Fudge's reasoning. But that was the logic Jane's parents had expected them to use....

Carissa glanced at Jane's mother, who was smiling as Macara pronounced her dead.

Varick's eyes turned gold. He looked at Alden. He commanded, "Do something, ankou."

Alden sank to the floor and closed his eyes. He placed both palms over Jane's body.

Too late, Carissa realized what was happening. "Wait!"

The color was already returning to Jane's face, and she breathed in deep gasps. Alden held her tight until her breathing calmed. Then, she opened her eyes and smiled.

"You brought me back to life, just as I knew you would." She hugged her brother.

"Of course, I did. I would never let anything happen to you."

"Of course, he did," Carissa repeated, feeling as if this whole situation had to be unreal. "Just as you knew he would. You knew he wouldn't let anything happen to Jane. You counted on him saving her." She looked at 'Jane' as Alden helped what should have been his sister to her feet.

"Why are you addressing her like that?" Varick asked.

Jane's smile twisted. She reached out for Varick, who pulled her up into his arms. "She thinks I'm Maeb. But you know who I am, don't you?" She caressed Varick's cheek. The gold flecks in Varick's eyes flickered. He searched her face. Before he could look into her eyes, she pulled him into a kiss. He pulled back. It was clear to everyone now.

This was not Jane.

Maeb, in Jane's body, laughed. She touched the edge of her lip and *tsked* in classic Maeb style. "You had to go and ruin it, Carissa." Her eyes traced Varick's form, up and down, "Too bad. How I would have liked to play Jane for you." She turned her attention to Cameron, telling Carissa, "Your man isn't bad, either. I'd have gladly taken your form. I knew Alden would have saved either of you." She held two hands up, weighing her empty palms like a scale. "His sister or the woman he loves. Either one would have worked for me. I might have let Alden think you loved him, too, if I were you. Two men are so much better than one."

Carissa's lips curled. "You're contemptible."

"You tricked me." Alden's hands turned to fists. Instead of the black of his eyes, his shifted to his skeletal form. He looked at his hands, then at Maeb, who looked very pleased with herself.

Maeb held up two fingers. "Twice. Or, I guess I tricked you three times if you count your becoming ankou in the first place. Now, let's see. If I still have my Tuatha de Danann magic, and your wraith powers now, I should be able to...." Maeb closed her eyes. She waved her palms over her face and torso. Her image changed from that of Jane's to that of Maeb's impression. She rolled her neck, and moaned. "Ah, yes. I feel like my old self again."

"It's just an illusion. This is still Jane's body. You can still save your sister, Alden," Macara said.

Tonics and Turning Points

"Ugh, always interfering," Maeb sneered. She perked up when her eyes landed on Raven at the outer doors. "Ah, my old friend. You've returned."

Raven scowled, "Everly is bound and handled. Looks like the witch is alive. Which of you made that mistake?"

Maeb snapped her fingers, "Right, that reminds me." She floated the talisman to Fudge's neck. The clasp buckled with a snap. "Thank you so much, sisters, for turning the talisman into a magic seal. It gives me such peace of mind knowing your powers are locked."

"There are more of us on the island," Fudge said.

"Yes, I know. I'll steal all your magic once I get used to this new body."

"You are outnumbered, Maeb," MacLir said.

"Yes, but you don't want Jane to die, so you won't harm her body. No, you're going to release the Everlys, walk out of this mansion, and reschedule Carissa's big day for tomorrow, and we'll all celebrate the start of a brand, new, wonderful life together. Won't we?"

Chapter 19

The Big Day

A blanket of snow covered the ground, glistening as the sun shone in the morning. It should not have been sunny. There should have been grey skies to match Carissa's stormy heart. Her dress should be ruined, given the torment it went through yesterday. But that had been in the Borderlands. Nothing from there affected the living world—except for Maeb.

Carissa clutched her herb-filled locket, the one she wore every day except the one before. Her mother's magic in her pendant made her feel protected, more so than the talisman that had both saved her and drained her of her powers. Though, she had no reason to feel safe now, she shouldn't be feeling like this, like it was the end of the world, on her wedding day. Yet, as she stared out the window at the sunny skies, she felt she was seeing Moss Hill as it was for the last time. If they failed today, the world would be forever changed.

A knock disturbed her thoughts. She peeked through the door to see Raven in a blue dress, her hair done up in a French braid. She was holding Carissa's bridal bouquet and looked more feminine than Carissa had ever seen her, and beautiful, too, in her own way. But now wasn't the time for compliments. She let Raven in. Chaos, Hiya, and Cynth followed. They surrounded Carissa's cheeks and neck, hugging her tight with enough magic and faerie dust flowing from them to warm her heart. She hugged them back.

"Thank you," she said as they let go.

"Nervous?" Raven asked.

Carissa closed the door. "How can I not be? Is she here?"

"Yes, and she's back in Jane's form. Despicable creature."

Carissa's fingers knotted together, "Are you sure this will work?"

Raven put a sympathetic hand on Carissa's whitening knuckles. "No, but it's all we could think up last night."

Carissa dropped her hands. Raven wasn't good at reassurances, but her bluntness did force Carissa to focus on the tasks at hand.

"Drink this." Raven handed her a tonic that had been tucked into the flowers in her hand.

Carissa took it and gulped it down. It tasted like fresh air after a spring rain. "Wow, I didn't expect that to taste so good."

Raven took the bottle back. "I'll take that as a compliment."

"Sorry."

"No problem. Now, are you ready to do your part?"

Carissa nodded. Cameron, though he must have been in pain after sharing the effects of the poison with her, had stayed up all night in an emergency brainstorming session with the Sidhe Council. The Redwood council room, apparently, was the only place in Moss Hill where Maeb couldn't spy through a glass. Of course, Macara, MacLir, and Raven had joined them. Reg and Maren, too, had stayed as long as they could.

But Carissa had been drained, powerless, and still healing. So, she'd left mid-way through the night to sleep at her parents' home in Vale. Raven had woken her early in the morning to take her to the Redwood and explain the plan. It was a good one. But whether it was enough to defeat Maeb was yet to be proven.

Raven handed her the bouquet and smoothed Carissa's hair, ensuring every strand was in place. "All set. Let's go."

Carissa closed her eyes, took a deep breath, in and out, and nodded. Every time she was reminded of the wedding, she felt a surge of joy, brought down again the next second by the fear of losing it all. Raven opened the door and Carissa walked to where her father stood, extending his arm for her to take. She wrapped her arm around his extra tighter. He placed his hand on hers, giving it a gentle, reassuring squeeze.

The "Bridal Chorus" played. Carissa walked in rhythm to the song, looking at the guests in attendance. How many of them knew the danger looming? She was surprised to see Hela, grinning and waving, and her husband, Fen, smiling beside her. Surely, Head Elf Roland wouldn't have wanted her in any danger? Thankfully, they had left the baby at home.

All of Carissa's friends and family had come, filling every chair. There was Cameron's family on the other side of the aisle, including his friends from school and city council. Even Belkin, whom Cameron must have invited just yesterday smiled and nodded as Carissa passed.

And there were the Everlys, impeccably dressed and sitting in the second row behind Cameron's parents. Fudge sat near them, the talisman still on his neck and him looking miserable. Raz, beside him held his hand. He made more than one glance of disgust toward the Everlys. Their haughty smiles sent a surge of magic through Carissa's blood, but she pushed it back, keeping her emotions in check. The audacity of the trio, to think themselves invincible in a room of magic-filled Mossies.

What was worse was perhaps they were right. No one in this town would want to hurt Jane, and even if it came to that, Maeb and the Everlys were still be more powerful than regular Mossies, fae included. Macara and MacLir sat in the front row on Carissa's side, directly opposite of Maeb. Raven took her seat beside them and gave Carissa one last encouraging look.

At the end of the aisle, Dorian shook hands with Cameron, kissed Carissa's cheek, and sat in the front row beside her mother. Maren took the bouquet, and Carissa put her hands in Cameron's. They were strong, and firm, and reassuring, and the look in Cameron's eyes made her believe that everything was going to be okay.

"Dearly beloved," Father Quinn began.

Carissa focused on Cameron's face, his eyes, his smile, the strength of his belief in their plan, all of it kept her emotions and magic from jolting to her fingertips or coming out in swirling clouds around her. If the magic overwhelmed her now, all would be lost.

"Do you, Cameron Larke, take Carissa Shae to be your lawfully wedded wife?"

Cameron responded confidently, "I do."

Carissa felt tears stinging. She could feel the love radiating from Cameron, the pinpoint focus he had on her despite everything else happening around them. He said "I do," but he meant, *"I love you, always, deeply, and forever."* For a moment, his love felt stronger than her fear. When her time came to say "I do," she let herself say it the way she would have yesterday, with nothing but love in her heart.

Father Quinn said, "I now pronounce you husband and wife. You may kiss the bride."

Cameron stepped forward. His arm captured the small of Carissa's back. His hand caressed her cheek and he looked directly into his eyes before their smiles locked into a kiss. Carissa felt a rush of magic and love flow through her, Cameron received all of it passionately.

Tabitha, unused to social norms, stood and cheered. It took her a minute to realize that she was the only one clapping and whistling. She looked around, turned a deep shade of green, and sat.

Carissa and Cameron's faces reddened and they smiled, turning around to make their way back down the aisle. If her eyes hadn't caught Maeb's on her way out she might have forgotten she was there to spoil her joy. At the door to the church, guests congratulated the happy couple, starting with those in the front row.

Maeb walked up to Carissa, extending a hand. Out of the corner of her eye, Carissa could see Cameron shaking Mr. Everly's hand, then greeting Mrs. Everly.

"Congratulations on your marriage," Maeb said as she held Carissa in an icy grip. She leaned forward, adding, "Let's hope it lasts as long as your grandfather's did."

Carissa's jaw set and her eyes narrowed. She tightened her handhold. Carissa's grandfather had died in much the same way as Alden. And they'd used the same excuse: pneumonia. She'd always thought it suspicious. Maeb all but confirmed that it was her doing. Was it Paden Finlay who had killed him? She wanted to ask, but Maeb had the upper hand at the moment and Carissa could say nothing for now. She had to let go. Maeb smirked, looked her up and down and dismissed Carissa with her eyes. Then, she continued out of the church.

Carissa shook Mr. and Mrs. Everly's hands. She pulled Fudge into a quick embrace, which he didn't resist.

Raz came after him, crying. "Carissa," he began, but she put a hand near his lips and shushed him.

"Everything will be fine," she said.

And as soon as he was gone, she looked at Cameron to confirm it. He nodded. As they continued shaking hands with guests, Carissa looked down the pavement, following the Everlys with her eyes until they disappeared among the cars.

A blast in the parking lot provoked screams among guests. A car flipped in the air, landing atop another in a fiery explosion. Macara, Raven, and MacLir ran to the front of the church. Once they were outside, Cameron stood in front of the double doors with his arms extended.

"Dorian, Reg," he called out. "Get these doors shut."

Carissa could hear her father commanding, "Remain calm. Please stay inside. It will be safer."

Tonics and Turning Points

Carissa and Cameron linked hands and ran to the parking lot. Macara, Raven, and MacLir had Maeb surrounded. Fudge and Raz had the Everlys cornered at their overturned limo. Mr. Everly focused on two cars on opposite sides of a row. Metal groaned against his pull, but could not resist him. Two cars crashed together, smashing Fudge and Raz between them. Glass shattered and fell to the ground like rain.

Carissa shouted, "Watch out," as her hands shot up. She pulled the metal back. The two cars fell to the ground. The view cleared to reveal the Rhys Dwfen pair unscathed. The hoods were bent in. They hadn't touched Fudge or Raz.

The Everlys however, were already attempting an escape. Fudge and Raz reached their hands out and tripped them with their magic. The sight was a blinding flash of light, like electricity had been tamed into a lasso and roped around their ankles. It dragged the two, screaming, back to them. The magic left burns on their ankles when Fudge and Sal finally let go.

"Hold still!" came a yell from the row ahead. The sound of hooves on pavement thundered from all sides. Dozens of sidhe guards, some on foot, some riding on horses, came toward them. The sound of Moss Hill police sirens blared from Greenfield Road.

Maeb began laughing. With one flick of a hand, she flung the sidhe guards closest to her to the ground. Varick leapt off his horse and hid behind a car as the sidhe around him skidded back. Maeb's grey mist filled the air.

She left a circle open around herself and the major players. With a look, Fudge and Raz were brought to their knees. They grasped their throats, gasping. Then, they, too, fell into the mist, unseen.

"I've got them." Macara ran into the mist behind them, leaving Raven and MacLir behind.

MacLir said, "Give up, Maeb. It's two Tuatha de Danann against one."

"Three," Carissa said.

"Two, three." She batted a hand in the air. Stopping, she smiled devilishly at Cam. "Even with one gorgeous human in the mix, you're no match for me." Her form changed and, as she had last night, resumed her true image. Looking like herself again, Maeb said, "Did you think I couldn't see Jane gathering magic from the people in Moss Hill? Or you Raven, giving it to her in a tonic this morning? Did you really think all their magic would be enough to stop me?"

"Jane's magic was stronger than yours," Carissa managed.

"Because that magic was connected to this body. Magic foreign to the body is difficult to control. You can feel that can't you with your borrowed Mossie magic. You can't handle it. I was just waiting to see you try to use it on me. Come on, try it against me. You can't wield it. But don't worry, I'll relieve you of the burden of it."

"Trust yourself, Carissa," MacLir said.

"Go ahead," Raven urged.

Carissa put her hand up and let the magic within her flow. It came out in waves of bright, burning light, a mix of pink and white. Maeb put her hands out to greet the magic. She grasped it and walked forward. Not only was she absorbing it, she was overpowering Carissa.

"Cari!" Cameron yelled from behind her as she fell to the ground.

Maeb climbed atop her, pushing her hands closer and closer to Carissa's heart. Carissa's hands flew to Maeb's arms. The magic was no longer flowing through her fingertips, but being drained into Maeb's hands. Maeb drew it out like lighting from a bottle. It sizzled and cracked as it rushed from her chest. Carissa's lungs felt afire. Her ribs felt like they were breaking. But the pain ended abruptly when Maeb's hand was pulled away.

Maeb looked at her hands. The glow around them faded in seconds. "This is all the town's magic? This is nothing."

Tonics and Turning Points

She tried to grab for more, but her hand stopped in midair. Her arm was held in place. She grunted, pulling against some unseen force. Try as she might, her hand wouldn't budge.

Carissa smiled. "Sorry, my heart is protected."

Maeb tried to pull her hand free, to reach Carissa's chest. She tried with her other arm, but that, too, hovered in midair. "Aargh! Whose magic dares to stop me?"

Maeb turned around to see Cameron, holding a palm out to her. His magic was invisible but the effect was there, pulling at her arms. "You? How? You have no magic."

Carissa replied, "He has all the Mossie magic—mine, the elves, the sidhe, the humans, the Tuatha de Danann, and more." She lifted herself so that her lips were close to Maeb's ear and whispered, "I sealed it in his heart with a kiss."

Maeb kicked Carissa back as she stood. Cameron still held her hands with his magic, but, as she walked toward him, it was difficult to tell who had whom in their grasp. Maeb meant to be intimidating, smiling as she neared Cameron, but he stayed in place. The disturbance in the air between them became enflamed in unnatural light, yellow on Cameron's side, red on Maeb's.

The yellow burned to orange as the red grew closer. Cameron yelled, leaning further into the magic. As he pushed back, the light became white-hot on Cameron's side. Once again, the air around his hands became invisible. The fog around him began to clear. The Mossie magic threatened to overtake Maeb entirely.

"You're doing it, you're winning!" Carissa said.

Maeb put one foot behind her, bracing against the force. She grunted and heaved her powers at him. Varick emerged from the fog behind him, sword in hand, as the reddish beam shot from Maeb's hands.

Varick ran to the center of the beam, slicing before the magic could travel any further. It erupted back at Maeb, throwing her to the ground in a swirling tornado of magic. It electrified the air around Maeb and her eyes glowed as she stood.

Maeb laughed. "Do you know how many lifetimes I've had to steal magic in this world and the next? I am more powerful than any magic this town has ever seen. I—" She stopped. A look of distress came over her face.

The magic around her dissipated. The force of wind around her remained, tousling her hair until the air stilled again. She looked at her hands, sparks of red, wisps of grey, and then nothing more than a sort of static electricity were all that was left. Panic took over her eyes and she looked at Cameron and Varick questioningly. The panic was replaced by pain as she put her hands to her face and cried out.

Carissa walked to Cameron. She stood behind him and placed a hand on his shoulder. He opened his arms to her and waved the others over to stand by them. Fudge, Raz, Varick, the sprites, and the Tuatha de Danann joined them. Macara and Raven wrapped their magic around Maeb's wrists, doubly binding her. MacLir summoned Alden.

Maeb placed her tied hands to her heart and groaned. "What have you done to me?"

Carissa answered, "The magic you stole from me—that was Jane's. She has her power back now. And I believe her body is now rejecting your foreign magic and awaiting the return of its true owner."

Maeb fell to her knees. Sidhe guards formed a half-circle around her. "How?" Maeb's eyes welled and reddened, bloodshot and frightened.

Carissa said, "You were watching all of us in this world and the next, who you thought might pose a threat to you. But your biggest flaw was that you ignored those you who thought were weak. And, who do you think are the weakest of all? The sprites. But Chaos is as strong as me and as clever as Raven. She can summon Alden from the World Beyond and he can take her there."

"You're saying a sprite gathered Jane's magic for you? Now I know you're lying. A sprite can't hold a druid's magic."

"I disagree. But just to be sure, we sent three."

Right on time, the sprites found their way out of the fog toward Carissa. They sat on her shoulders, arms crossed, and staring Maeb down.

Maeb laughed as if she found it all too amusing. "Their hug! They transferred Jane's magic to you in a hug? How precious. You're still bluffing. Jane is locked up tight and this time there's no way you can get to her."

"She *was* locked up in the Redwood you use as your prison hold in the Borderlands." Alden appeared through a black mist of his own. He tossed a shard of stone at Maeb's feet. "You made it harder by breaking the portal. I found another way in."

"Persistent. But the tree has no entrance like it does in Vale, and it heals itself. What did you do, spend all night attacking the tree with your magic to get in and then all morning doing the same to get out? You must be exhausted," Maeb said. All smugness left her face as multiple forms appeared in the mist.

Miss Morgan, Toffee, Otto Crimbal, and several other Mossies took a ghostlike shape before her. One of them, a man Carissa recognized only from photographs in Nan's albums, stood in front of them all. Maeb's eyes watered and her lips trembled.

It made her look pathetic, and Alden responded with contempt, "You and your followers might be willing to sacrifice family members for power, but some of us are still loyal to those we love."

"Touching." Maeb said. Her breath was labored now. "Some of us are loyal to a cause. You think this will stop me or my followers? I'll only try again or they will for me."

MacLir said, "Your followers will be weak without you, Maeb. And you most certainly *cannot* try again. Once you're gone from Jane's body, you'll no longer have any part of your soul in a vessel in the living world. And, as for the powers you stole, you may have been able to keep them in the Borderlands, but you'll find the World Beyond is a different story. I believe you'll be visited by many spirits this night, who will be taking those powers back from you once you're dead."

Maeb's face was changing now. Her ancient visage cracking, she touched her cheeks. Her fingers became wet from tears. She looked at Carissa with venom. "You will never truly be rid of me."

Carissa shuddered.

Cameron pulled her into his chest, so she could look away as the last of Maeb broke from Jane's body and fell as dust on the ground. Jane, now herself, fell to her knees. Varick rushed to catch her. He held her in his arms, brushed her hair back and smiled as her eyes fluttered open.

"Varick?" she said, weakly.

Varick held Jane as if he would never let go again. She cried into his shoulder as the sidhe guards took Mr. and Mrs. Everly away. Alden walked to his sister's side, refusing to look at his parents.

The forms of Mossies from the World Beyond faded from view. Carissa looked at her grandfather with gratitude. He smiled and nodded. In his eyes, she saw all the love he felt for her and knew the years that Maeb had taken from them could not have lessened their bond. She'd meet him one day, many years from now, in the World Beyond.

Carissa's parents rushed to embrace her. She wasn't sure if Nan had seen her grandfather, but she was crying as she hugged Carissa tight. The wedding guests came out of the church in a wave of questions, condolences, hugs, and happiness. Terrible as the destruction was, it was a good day, after all.

Reg clapped Cameron on the back. "I think you two deserve a reception after that."

Maren said, "The Rose Garden was all booked up for today, so Sal and Holly are preparing a reception, if you're up to it."

"Oh, let me tell him the next surprise, please!" Tabitha ran up to them, saying, "You're going to be my first customers!"

Tonics and Turning Points

Reg explained, "We know you missed the departure for your honeymoon cruise, so, Tabitha volunteered to open her Bed and Breakfast early for you. In fact, she's hosting the reception at her home."

Reg gave an uncertain look, but Tabitha was all smiles.

Cameron said, "Thank you, Reg, Maren. Today wasn't exactly the perfect wedding day we had pictured. I'm not sure if Cari wants to—"

Carissa touched his arm. She reached for a hug from Maren, Reg, and Tabitha, saying, "It's better than perfect. Maeb is gone forever, Jane is alive, Moss Hill is safe. I couldn't be happier."

Cameron took Carissa's hand and kissed it.

As they walked away, Macara appeared in front of Cameron and Carissa, arms crossed and blocking their path. "I believe you've forgotten something."

"The sprites!" Carissa said as she realized they were gone.

"More than that," Raven called out. She led Hiya, Cynth, and Chaos out of the church.

The sprites carried boxes filled with gift bags down the steps. Their faerie dust magic floated the boxes right to Cameron's feet. Raven picked up a bag.

"You have to give the magic back." She handed the bag to Cameron.

"Right. Of course, I was going to."

"In the gift bags?" Carissa asked.

"Why not?" Raven said. "All the classiest gift bags at weddings have a touch of magic in them. If you really want to impress your guests, let a little love flow from your heart along with it. Love always makes the best present."

Chapter 20

Happily Ever After

After two days at Tabitha's Vale Heights Bed and Breakfast and a seven day honeymoon cruise around the Atlantic, Carissa and Cameron returned home ready to embark on a new journey: their lives together as husband and wife. Their home would be ready and waiting for them in Vale woods and Cameron was eager to see it.

"You know it will still be there later today, maybe even tomorrow, too," Carissa joked.

Heaving their luggage into the trunk of the taxi, Cameron said, "I have a surprise I want to show you on the way there, get in."

Carissa sat in the car, unwrapping her scarf in the warm air of the cab. Cameron sat beside her and directed the driver to take them to Mount Vale. He could have had anything waiting for her, even just a trip to have lunch at Gooseberry Café, or spent an afternoon in her parents' home in Vale, and Carissa would have been ecstatic. Everything from Breakfast in Bed at Tabitha's to Christmas Eve on the cruise had been sweeter for sharing it with her husband.

Husband. How she loved the word. More so, she loved the man attached to it. Her bond with him was strong enough to bring her back to life and now she had a lifetime for that bond to grow even stronger.

Best of all was the gift of sharing this Christmas Day together in their own home. Covered in snow on a clear winter day, Moss Hill was a sight only Mossie eyes could fully appreciate. Especially when they turned on the path to Mount Vale, the scene became truly spectacular.

Carissa used her double-sight to see into the Otherworld and human worlds at the same time. She could see the faerie fire smoke from fae homes rising above Vale in their various colors and the twisting paths that led to Vale and to Tabitha's home and to Cam and Carissa's home, as well. But the car did not turn down any of those paths.

Instead of heading left, the car turned right, down the road to Fairfield Castle. Carissa raised an eyebrow. Cameron smiled. When they neared the castle, he escorted her out of the car and up to the gate. Taking out a small envelope that Carissa had thought was nothing more than a friendly note their friends had sent them on their cruise, Cameron slid out a key. He unlocked the gate and they entered the grounds.

Carissa marveled at the reconstruction. There were no half-caved-in walls, no cobwebs or broken windows. Instead, it was smooth, silver walls, clean, shining windows and a banner that read: *Camp Larke: A Cultural Exchange.*

"It was your project that won the castle?" Carissa asked.

Cameron smiled. "I am the liaison between Vale and Moss Hill, after all—even if it's not official anymore. I gave my proposal to the bank and got a start-up loan. Mrs. O'Brien agreed to lease the castle to me, with the option to own it eventually."

"So, this summer, you're officially in business?"

"The camp opens in the summer. My job starts right after the holiday. We have to prepare this place to be a haven for kids from every fae race and humans from all walks of life to come together and create lifelong friendships. I've already got applicants worldwide. I'm going to have to sift through the applications and choose the ones best suited to spread the Mossie message."

"And what message is it we'll be spreading?" Carissa asked, already knowing the answer.

"This castle was once a place where wars were planned and fought. It's fitting that we use it now to plan a peaceful future. It's time for people to see each other for who we all really are and what we can be together. The time for division is over. The worlds are ready to unite."

Carissa and Cameron stood there a long while, admiring the castle and all it represented. It struck her as a turning point in the war against the unseelie. Carissa still worried that, unintentionally, the Mossie message would make Moss Hill all the more a target for unseelie who didn't like the vision of unity among fae and humans. But the time for secrets was over, which meant the time for vigilance had just begun. She was ready to help protect the good work Cameron planned to do. And she knew others would be willing to protect his vision, too. It was a much better plan for Moss Hill than Maeb could have ever dreamed.

The thought of her still haunted the darkest part of Carissa's mind. But as they drove back through the Vale woods, with Cameron's arm around her in the warmth of the cab, she could see the woods in in a completely different light. When their home came into view, Carissa felt her elf-light tingling. It wasn't just the excitement of being home.

Her elf ears caught the sound of muffled voices even before they reached the door. Cameron caught sight of a light turning off and a bit of faerie dust strewn across the *Welcome* mat gave away what lay inside. Cameron and Carissa nodded at one another before they swung the door open wide and waited for their friends to yell *"Surprise!"*

"Welcome home!" Tabitha yelled, out of sync with the others. Faerie dust rained over them, courtesy of three overzealous sprites. Carissa's parents wrapped them both in hugs. Cameron's parents did the same.

Nan said, "I'm glad you're both home. Those sprites are difficult to handle without you, Cari."

Carissa laughed and gave her grandmother an appreciative hug. The sprites joined in, pressing their arms against Carissa's neck and cheeks. A tugging at her pant leg made Carissa look down.

A baby in a solid, blue onesie pulled himself upright but then plopped onto his knees again. He giggled and tried again.

"Why, hello there," Cameron knelt down and picked the boy.

"What's your name?" Carissa asked.

"Hamish Otto Crimbal. I decided he needed a name of his own and I've always thought it would be neat to have a middle name," Tabitha said. She took her baby into her arms. "I told you he was cute, didn't I? I just love this button nose! I hate to brag, but I think I sculpted him just perfect."

The boy had a beautiful smile, glowing, green eyes and dark hair. His skin was dark like his fathers, but that was where the resemblance ended. Carissa was sure she'd seen the face in a children's clothing catalog or some such thing before. Knowing Tabitha, she'd chosen a baby picture she liked and worked from memory.

Regardless of how he was born, the baby was a bundle of joy. Carissa pulled Tabitha in for a congratulatory hug and added, "I think he's wonderful."

Hela, appearing beside them with her own beautiful baby girl, said, "I think Tabitha made him a bit big for his age, walking already and only a day old."

"Is he advanced already?" Tabitha nearly jumped for joy, literally lifting on her toes.

"I'm telling you he's going to be a handful," Hela said.

"I think he'll be wonderful," Cameron said.

"And your little one is looking radiant. Have you named her yet?"

It was really getting quite ridiculous, having a child already two weeks old and nameless. But Hela required perfection and that meant taking time. She rocked her sleeping beauty in her arms as she said, "We chose a human name: Gemstone. Gem for short. What do you think?"

It wasn't exactly a human name, not a common one, anyway, but it was unique and somehow fitting for the little one in Hela's arms.

Carissa gave her a congratulatory hug and when the proud father walked over, Cameron shook his hand. "Congratulations, Fen. And thank you for designing this stunning home."

With a hug for Fen, Carissa added, "Yes, thank you. We're so grateful to be in our own home for Christmas, too."

"It really is a lovely, house, isn't it, Reg?" Maren said, walking over with her arm around Reg's waist and a drink in her hand.

The enormous grin gave it away the second Carissa saw her, but so did the diamond on her finger. Carissa reached for a hug, exclaiming, "You're engaged!"

"Looks like everyone has something to congratulate today," Cameron teased, "And I couldn't be happier for you."

When Cameron offered his hand, Reg pulled him into a hug, "I don't think I could be happier, either, except if everyone was inside the party." Reg nodded toward the sliding doors leading out back.

Cameron turned around.

Carissa did, too. The lights on the back patio dimly lit the yard so that she could make out a distant form in the window. Alden was standing alone at the edge of their garden.

"Remind you of something?" Cameron asked.

Carissa recalled a garden party at Roland's a year ago, when she and Cameron had caught sight of Alden standing apart from the crowd. That was before Jane knew he was an ankou, before the townsfolk knew anything of the unseelie, the World Beyond, or Maeb. It was a simpler time and lonelier for Alden than it needed to be now.

"Would you excuse us?" Carissa said.

Tonics and Turning Points

Hand in hand, Cameron and Carissa walked out the sliding doors and made their way across the snow.

"What are you doing alone again this time?" Carissa asked.

"I wasn't sure I'd be welcome." Alden made quick glances at her and Cameron. "I've lost my wraith powers, but I'm still an ankou. I just wanted to see that everyone was safe, but I think I should go." He began to fade.

Carissa put a hand on his wrist and held his gaze. "You're not the ankou to us, you're a Mossie. Always were, always will be."

"Not just a Mossie, our friend, Alden." Cameron put his hand out. Alden shook it with a smile, which broke into a grin when Cameron pulled him in for a hug.

"Alden?" Jane walked out the sliding doors. The nature faeries, Hiya and Cynth, flew to Cameron and Carissa's shoulders respectively. Their little bodies shivered and Carissa felt Cynth lean against her like an icicle touching her neck.

"Why are we out here?" Varick asked, "Ankou, can you not join us inside or must you insist that we freeze out here? You may not feel the cold, but your sister does." He wrapped an arm around Jane and she leaned into his chest.

"Sorry," Alden said.

"You shouldn't be sorry, you should be inside with us. Making us come out here to you, it's really—"

"Not a bother," Macara said.

"Not a bother at all. Why are we out here?" Barnaby asked.

"Oh, here if you must whine like children." Raven waved an arm up over her head and down to her feet. It looked like nothing happened, but as they walked closer, Carissa could feel the bubble of heated air radiating around the group. Once directly in front of her, Raven pulled Carissa into a hug. Cari stiffened, eyes wide, but slowly relaxed into returning the gesture.

"What was that for?" she asked as they parted. Raven had never seemed like the hugging type. And was she teary-eyed or was that just Carissa's imagination?

Raven touched Carissa's face like a mother to a child. "My work here is done." Patting her cheek twice, Raven let go.

Carissa said, "You did swear to protect Maeb's descendants, didn't you?"

"I promised to protect your grandfather's line for Maeb but ended up protecting them from her. And now she's gone and you're safe and I've kept my word."

"You sent Chaos to me because of your promise?"

Chaos hugged Raven with love and faerie dust swirling around them. Then Chaos let go floated over to Carissa and Cameron. Hiya hugged her and twirled and Cynth invited her to sit with her on Carissa's open shoulder.

Raven nodded. "And it looked like Chaos has chosen to stay."

"But you're going," Carissa said.

"I've become so very fond of this place—but there's a whole wide world that needs me."

Carissa remembered Raven's tales of wild jungles and giant spiders and fae and humans whom she had met in her journeys. She loved danger and the thrill of helping people out of it—that was her life.

"And what about you?" Carissa looked to MacLir, Macara, and Holly.

MacLir stepped back, "I'm only here for the celebration. But you know I'm a ferry boat away in Scotland should you need me."

Macara said, "And I'll stay until Jane and Varick return from their trip."

"Your trip?" Cameron asked.

Jane clutched the tree amulet around her neck. "I'm going to Tara, to make sure our link with the World Beyond is broken and that Maeb's soul has no way of returning. I've also inherited the family business, which means that I'll be traveling often now to oversee our work."

"What about being Moss Hill's protector?" Carissa asked.

Varick said, "I think it is clear to all of us that you share that role with Jane."

Jane added, "Besides, if Moss Hill is going to become a center for a movement uniting human and fae, then the best way for us to protect it is to strengthen our alliances with other places like ours. I plan to make all of my travels a double purpose, to strengthen Moss Hill's economy and secure its future."

"You'll be great, Jane. I can't imagine the job in better hands," Alden said.

Jane smiled sadly, "I can. But then I still have you here, in your way, to help."

"Whenever you need m."

"You have all of us, Jane, and you, Carissa, too. I will come and go, but Holly will be here, keeping my home in order for the times when I return."

"Barnaby and I are always here for you, my dears."

Barnaby said, "I should hope so, Carissa's counting on you for the morning shift at the Seelie Tree Apothecary shop tomorrow."

Carissa and Holly laughed.

As hugs were exchanged, Reg opened the sliding door. "Come inside, all of you. They want a Christmas toast with the newlyweds."

Cameron wrapped an arm around Carissa, gave Alden a friendly push on his back, and led the group forward.

Indoors, glasses of elderberry wine sat on the dining table. Cameron handed glasses to Alden, Jane, and Varick. The others all took theirs.

Then, taking a glass for Carissa and himself, he said, "You all know about our struggles with Maeb and the unseelie this past year. We've had our losses." He looked at Tabitha. Then looking at little Hamish and Gemstone, he added, "And we've had new additions to our families. We've faced obstacles none of us could have faced alone and victories we brought about together. We now know that we are strong enough together to face anything." He looked at Jane, Varick, and Alden. "And that our connections to each other are stronger than even death could tear asunder." He looked at Reg and Maren, leaning into each other, bursting with joy as they listened to his speech. Then at the rest of their friends: Fudge and Raz, Sal, the Larkes, the Shaes, the Harbridges, Head Elf Roland and his wife, and even some of the sidhe and elves from the councils. Cameron took Carissa's hand and kissed it. "Most importantly, I can see now that Moss Hill is overflowing with the most powerful magic in any world. Love has overcome hate and led to a new beginning for Moss Hill." He raised his glass. "To new beginnings."

"To new beginnings," Carissa said along with the others.

"And to a Merry Christmas!" Clarence shouted, picking up a glass of the elderberry wine.

Barnaby snatched it from his cousin's hand and switched it with an elderberry juice. Then, he added, "And many happy new years!"

~The End~

Or is it the beginning?

Want more great content?

Hi, I'm Astoria Wright, the author of The Faerie Apothecary Cozy Mysteries. I hope you've enjoyed the first book in this series.

Check out the rest of
The Faerie Apothecary Mysteries:

Chaos in the Countryside
Herbs and Homicide
Remedy and Ruins
Elixirs and Elves
Charms and Changelings
Potions and Panic
Talismans and Turmoil
Tonics and Turning Points

To keep up with this series and others by the author, check out the website:

www.astoriawright.com

Sign up for the mailing list for updates and freebies available only to members!

A Note from Chaos:

Do you like this book?
I hope you do.
Please do me a favor
and leave a review!

Thanks for reading!